# RUBY
## Reinvented

# RUBY
## Reinvented

### By Ronni Arno

ALADDIN M!X

New York  London  Toronto  Sydney  New Delhi

This book is a work of fiction. Any references to historical events, real people, or real places are used fictitiously. Other names, characters, places, and events are products of the author's imagination, and any resemblance to actual events or places or persons, living or dead, is entirely coincidental.

ALADDIN M!X

Simon & Schuster Children's Publishing Division

1230 Avenue of the Americas, New York, New York 10020

First Aladdin M!X edition November 2015

Text copyright © 2015 by Ronni Arno Blaisdell

Cover illustration copyright © 2015 by Lucy Truman

Also available in an Aladdin hardcover edition.

All rights reserved, including the right of reproduction in whole or in part in any form.

ALADDIN is a trademark of Simon & Schuster, Inc., and related logo is a registered trademark of Simon & Schuster, Inc.

ALADDIN M!X and related logo are registered trademarks of Simon & Schuster, Inc.

For information about special discounts for bulk purchases, please contact Simon & Schuster Special Sales at 1-866-506-1949 or business@simonandschuster.com.

The Simon & Schuster Speakers Bureau can bring authors to your live event. For more information or to book an event contact the Simon & Schuster Speakers Bureau at 1-866-248-3049 or visit our website at www.simonspeakers.com.

Book designed by Laura Lyn DiSiena

The text of this book was set in Anglecia Pro.

Manufactured in the United States of America 1015 OFF

10 9 8 7 6 5 4 3 2 1

Library of Congress Control Number 2015940919

ISBN 978-1-4814-3757-8 (hc)

ISBN 978-1-4814-3756-1 (pbk)

ISBN 978-1-4814-3758-5 (eBook)

For Hallie & Morgan

# RUBY
## *Reinvented*

# Chapter
## ★ 1 ★

BEST. PARTY. EVER.

I'm pretty sure being twelve will be my most fabulous age yet, even though there are still three days until my *actual* birthday.

"Hey, Ruby." Sophie holds up an empty bowl. "Got any more of these awesome chips?"

"Of course." I take the chip bowl and flash Sophie my brightest BFF smile. She smiles back. It's kinda weird how she looks right past me, like she's looking for someone else, but whatever. Sophie's been my best friend all year, ever since we started middle school. We like the same books, the same movies, and we're both totally in love with the color orange. I mean, how many people truly love the color orange? It's fate. I'm sure of it.

I weave in and out of a sea of friends, chip bowl in hand. Someone turns the music up, and dancing and laughing fill the room. I walk just a little bit taller as I realize that all these people are here for me—to celebrate my birthday, the first real birthday party I've ever had.

Someone brushes against my arm as I walk by, and the chip bowl wobbles in my hands when I see who it is.

Damon Gorman.

"Where ya going?" Damon's big brown laser-beam eyes stare right at me, and I think I might pass out—right here at my own birthday party.

"Uhh, chips." I hold up the empty bowl.

"Cool." He nods and gives me his famous Damon Gorman smile, perfect with bright white teeth and deep dazzling dimples. He stares at me a couple of seconds longer and then turns away.

I'm still standing there, knees shaking and palms sweating. *Uhhhh, chips.* Real cool, Ruby. Real cool. For six months I've been dying to talk to Damon Gorman, and those are the bewitching words that sprout from my mouth.

I practically fly down the marble staircase. Seriously, I don't feel my feet touching the floor. It's a good thing, too, since we have a lot of stairs. Thirty-eight to be exact. I want to get down to the kitchen as quickly as possible so I can get back up to the party room.

Ellie is in the kitchen with a few other people who work

at our house. She turns the water off and wipes her hands on a dish towel as I come in.

"What do you need, Bea?" Everyone in my family calls me Bea, because when I was little I couldn't pronounce Ruby. Ellie says Ruby especially funny, since she rolls her *r*'s. Some of my friends have a hard time understanding her, but since Ellie's been with our family since I was a baby, I'm used to her Russian accent.

I hold up the bowl. "More chips, please."

She takes the chip bowl from my hand and fills it up. "Here you go, bubela."

"Thanks, Ellie." I skip out of the kitchen. "You're the best!"

I head back up the stairs, slowly now that chips are spilling out over the top of the bowl, and toward the party room. It's supposed to be a library, but since my parents are too busy to read much, they use it for entertaining. The room opens up to a really big deck that overlooks the beach, so guests seem to like it. The music is lower now, and my friends have divided into little groups. Some are at the food table, where I drop off the bowl of chips, some are messing around with their iPhones, and some are out on the deck. I spot Sophie out there with a bunch of other people and notice that Damon is one of them. I floof up my hair and open the double doors that lead outside. Sophie and Damon are standing closest to the doors, their backs toward me.

"I don't think they're here tonight," Sophie says to Damon.

"Have you ever met them?" Damon asks.

"No. I've only seen them from a distance, when they came for parent-teacher conferences. It's driving me crazy! I mean, how long do I have to act like Ruby's best friend?"

I freeze.

Damon shrugs. "She's not all that bad. She throws good parties."

"Sure, but other than that she's dullsville. For six months I've been bored out of my mind, waiting to meet them. Plus, how much more orange can I possibly wear? I look awful in orange. Everybody looks awful in orange."

I can't breathe.

"I wouldn't mind meeting Zack. He could get me World Series tickets." Damon winks.

Sophie gives Damon a push. "Forget him! What about her? If she met me, she'd see I've totally got what it takes to be a supermodel. Couldn't you see me on next season's *America's Next Cover Model*? Lots of supermodels go on to be movie stars, too, you know, which of course is my ultimate goal."

Tears prick my eyes, and I blink hard.

"Well, they've got to show up sometime," Sophie says. "But maybe they think their daughter is as lame as I do. She stinks at sports. And she's not even that cute. I mean, how can you have a star baseball player as a dad and a super-model as a mom and be so—talentless?"

*Talentless.*

I can't stop the tears now. They're streaming down my face. I'm practically blind as I fling open the double doors, run through the party room, and push my bedroom door open. I hurl myself inside, slam the door shut, and throw myself onto my bed.

Worst. Party. Ever.

# Chapter

## ★ 2 ★

ELLIE'S KNOCKING ON MY DOOR.

"Bea? Bea, are you in there?"

I know I can't ignore her. She'll freak out and call the police. Or worse. She'll call my parents.

I drag myself off the bed and open the door.

"Bea!" She puts her hand on my cheek. "Your guests are looking for you. What happened? Why you crying?"

"Oh, Ellie, it was horrible!" I turn away from her and plop down on my bed.

"Horrible? On your birthday? What could be so horrible, Bea?"

"I overheard my friends talking." I put the palms of my hands over my eyes. "They're only pretending to like me so they can meet Mom and Dad."

"What do you mean, bubela?" She sits down next to me on the bed. "Of course your friends like you."

"No they don't. I heard them talking. Sophie . . ." A sob clogs my throat, but I swallow it down. "Sophie said that I was lame and boring and she only wanted to hang out with me to meet my parents."

Ellie takes my hand. We sit in silence for a few minutes, until she stands up, smooths her apron, and looks down at me.

"Well then, bubela, they do not deserve you. If they cannot appreciate you for who you are, then they are missing out on a wonderful friend."

I give her a weak smile. "Thanks, Ellie, but what am I going to do? I can't go back out there. I never want to see them again."

Ellie points her finger in the air. "I will tell them you are sick, and then we do the FaceTime with your parents tonight and figure this out."

I nod. "Yes, tell them I'm sick. Because I am, Ellie. I am feeling sick."

Ellie leaves my room and I'm alone. I start pacing. There's no way I could face Sophie or Damon again. If they feel that way about me, probably everyone else does too. Everyone at school follows Sophie and Damon like sheep dressed in designer clothing. I'll say one thing, Sophie *should* be an actress. She could have won an Oscar for her performance as the Best Friend this last year. She totally had me fooled.

I hate her. And I hate this school. I wince when I think about going back to private tutoring. No way I can do that again. I just want to be a normal girl with normal friends. But there's nothing normal about my life.

There's only one solution. I have to switch schools.

Yes, that's it! I'll go someplace where nobody knows who my parents are. But how? My parents will have to come to school at some point, and then everyone will know that I'm the daughter of supermodel-turned–TV star Celestine Cruz and Los Angeles Dodgers star pitcher Zack Miller, who *People* magazine recently dubbed the Sexiest Man Alive. Gag.

Maybe if I could just get out of Hollywood. People here are star crazy, always trying to meet someone who could help their career. It won't be like that everywhere. I bet the farther I can get from Hollywood the better. I pull my iPad out of the desk drawer and search for a map of the United States. I find the point in the country that's the farthest away from Hollywood.

Maine.

I google boarding schools in Maine. There are only a few, and most of those are high schools. I have to find one that has a middle school, too.

Bingo.

Midcoast Academy. Grades six through twelve.

It's perfect. And it's 3,174 miles away.

Now I just have to convince my parents to let me live across the country for the next six years. Without them. Without Ellie. Without anyone we've ever met before, in a place we've never even been before, to a school I found on the Internet.

I sit on my bed and groan.

I'm not sure how long I'm there for, but it's dark outside by the time Ellie comes back in.

"Okay, Bea, they are all gone."

"Good."

"Sophie said to tell you she hopes you feel better."

"Right," I half say, half snort.

"Come on." She pats my knee. "It's time for the FaceTime."

"It's eight o'clock already?" I ask.

"Yes, so let's get the FaceTime set up, eh? We do not want to be late for your parents."

I click on the FaceTime icon. A few seconds later two boxes appear on my screen. Mom's face is in one box; Dad's face is in the other.

"Hi, baby," Mom says, beaming. She's still in full makeup, and her black curly hair is all sparkly. The *America's Next Cover Model* stylists like to put glitter in it before taping.

"Hi, Mom. Find the next top supermodel yet?"

"Oh, who knows. These auditions are grueling. And wow, is it cold up here in Wisconsin."

"Hey, you beautiful women. Don't leave me high and dry. Get it? High and dry? Because I'm in the desert?"

"Ha-ha, Dad." Dad has the worst jokes, but I smile anyway. "How's spring training going?"

"Hot! I'm ready to come home to easy breezy California. I can't wait until I can snuggle with my girls."

"Three more days," Mom says. She takes off her chandelier-size earrings. "You know we're always together on your birthday, Bea."

"Speaking of birthdays, how was your party today?" Dad asks.

"Oh, it was good." I just can't bear to tell them the truth right now. They'd be so upset for me, and I know how tired Mom is after a shoot. Dad looks exhausted from practicing all day.

"So, have you thought about what you want for your birthday?" Mom asks.

"Yeah, I think I have."

"Are you going to tell us?" Dad laughs after a long pause.

"Can I tell you when you get here?"

"But then we won't have it ready on time," Mom says.

"It's not that kind of present," I say.

"I'm intrigued." Dad smiles that famous smile of his, the one that makes the edges of his bright blue eyes all crinkly.

Sometimes I think he's more well-known for his smile than he is for his fastball. His nickname isn't the Pretty Pitcher for nothing.

"I'll tell you all about it when you get home," I say. "Only three more days."

And that's when I'll spring it on them. I'll tell them about Sophie and the party and Midcoast Academy. There's no way they'll be able to turn me down. It's the only birthday gift I'm going to ask for. They'll have to give it to me.

They'll have to.

# Chapter

## ★ 3 ★

I TALK ELLIE INTO LETTING ME STAY HOME ON Monday. She makes me go to school on Tuesday, but I figure I can fake it for one day.

My "friends" decorated my locker for my actual birthday, and when I get to school, they're all cheering and clapping. Sophie's leading the pack, of course.

"Happy birthday, bestie!" Sophie squeals, and gives me an air-kiss and a hug.

"Hey, Ruby." Damon puts his arm around my shoulder. I can't believe I actually liked him. Now instead of getting butterflies in my stomach when I look at him, I feel like I'm going to throw up. And not in the good way. "Happy birthday. I'm glad you're feeling better."

"Thanks." I channel my Mom and flash my best Celestine

Cruz smile. Maybe I did inherit the performing gene, because nobody can tell I'm faking. I'm not sure I can keep this up all day, though. By second period I'm exhausted. My head hurts, my cheeks hurt, and I'd really like to punch Sophie in the nose. I don't know how my parents do this for a living. Smile through the pain. That's what Mom says when she has to do a fashion show with a headache, or if she and her director argue just before a taping. I'm smiling so much today that I think my face might stick like this forever.

By lunch I'm totally fried.

"Hey, bestie." Sophie elbows me gently in the side. For a second I consider elbowing her back . . . only much harder. "You okay? You're so quiet today."

"Just tired I guess."

"Awwwww." She puts her arms around my shoulders and squeezes. I try not to flinch. Then she babbles on about how great my hair looks today (I didn't even brush it) and how we should totally go get matching mani/pedis over the weekend.

I somehow make it through the next few periods with my fake smile and my fake friends. When the bell finally rings for dismissal, I jump up, grab my stuff out of my locker, and head to the parking lot. Like a lot of kids, I take a car home.

"Hello, birthday girl!" Curtis is standing next to the limo. It's such a relief to see him, black suit pressed neatly as always, chauffeur's hat placed squarely on his head, and a huge smile as he opens the door for me. "How was your day?"

"It was okay." I climb into the backseat.

"Just okay? Anything special happen on your birthday?"

"My friends," I begin, barely choking the word out, "decorated my locker."

"Nice!" Curtis smiles at me in the rearview mirror.

"Do you know if Mom and Dad are home yet?"

"They might be," Curtis said. "Jimmy was scheduled to pick them up at two."

My parents have a lot of people who work for them. Curtis and Jimmy are the drivers. Curtis usually takes me to and from school, unless he's on vacation, and then Jimmy takes me. They're both really nice, but I like Curtis a tiny bit better. He seems to know when I don't feel like chatting, so he'll just keep quiet. Like now.

We pull up to our gated street and drive up the long, circular driveway. Jimmy's car is already there, so I practically leap out of Curtis's car before it even stops. Ellie must have heard us pull up, because she's already at the front door.

"Are they home?" I ask it so loudly that my voice echoes off the paving bricks.

Before Ellie can answer, Mom and Dad appear in the doorway.

"There's my baby!" Mom yells, and pulls me into her arms.

"Mom!" I squeeze her as tight as I can. She smells like vanilla and lavender, and her cashmere cardigan feels warm against my face. It's not a sweater I recognize. She's got it paired with black leggings and thigh-high boots. It's a good look, but then of course a supermodel *would* look like she stepped out of a fashion magazine. I just wish her clothing choices would be more . . . her.

Mom lets go, and Dad moves in for a bear hug. "Happy birthday, Bea."

"Thanks, Daddy." He's wearing his favorite brown leather jacket, which crinkles softly when I hug him.

"So," Mom says, her brown eyes shining. "I thought we could go to Sarriette's for dinner tonight.

"Sarriette's?" My stomach rumbles just thinking about it. Their ravioli is to die for. "You want to go out?"

"Well, it is your birthday." Mom brushes my hair behind my ear.

"Yeah, but you know what happens when we go out."

"I had my publicist call Sarriette's and ask them to give us a private room and let us in the back door. Nobody will even know we're there."

I bite my lower lip. Even when we try to sneak into places, someone somehow always finds out. Either some tourist with a cell phone snaps a picture, or the paparazzi jump out of the bushes. Mom and Dad are used to the attention, but they hate when photographers get in my face. I

have to admit—I hate it too. But thinking of Sarriette's ravioli trumps thinking of the annoying paparazzi, so I smile.

I put on a silver dress with sparkly spaghetti straps that
I made myself. It took me two months, but I think it's my best
one yet. Just deciding where to place the rhinestones took
weeks. I wanted to make sure they were sparkly enough to
be noticed, but not so sparkly that they took away from the
shine of the fabric.

I dig through my closet and find a pair of silver ballet
flats that match the dress perfectly. I leave my hair long and
loose, and when I glance in the mirror to put on some lip
gloss, I think that maybe I'm starting to look a little like Mom.
We have the same black curly hair and olive skin, but my
blue eyes and dimples come straight from Dad. I sigh. Who
am I kidding? Sophie was right. Somehow these features
look amazing on my parents, but when combined on my
face, they just look weird.

There's a knock on my bedroom door. I open it to find
Dad standing there, dressed in blue jeans, a white shirt, and
a black tie.

"Your chariot awaits, Bea." He bends his elbow, and I
slip my arm in his. We prance down the stairs and out to
the waiting car, my dress following me like a cloud of silver.
Jimmy is there, waiting for us to climb in.

"Where's your mother?" Dad asks me.

I shrug. "You know she takes forever to get ready."

"I'm coming, I'm coming," Mom calls from the front porch. Her heels are at least three inches tall, but she effortlessly glides down the porch stairs toward the waiting car. I look down at my ballet-slippered feet and decide that no matter how hard I try, I'll never be as glamorous or beautiful as her. Never.

Mom slides in next to me, and Jimmy closes the door behind her. He then makes his way to the driver's seat, and we roll down the driveway toward Sarriette's.

Nobody says anything about my dress. As usual. I shake off the slight sadness I feel. I'm sure if my parents weren't so busy, they'd notice my designs.

"Isn't this so nice?" Mom squeezes my arm with one hand and uses the other to look at her makeup in a compact mirror. "All of us together?"

I smile. We haven't been together in weeks. It's been like this since I was little, so I hardly remember any other way. Ellie takes care of me most of the time, and I FaceTime with my parents every night. I never realize just how much I miss them until they come back.

We pull into a dark parking lot, and the car stops at what I assume is the back door of Sarriette's. Jimmy gets out first, and Mom, Dad, and I stay in the car. He knocks on the door, and a guy in a suit steps outside and talks with him. He nods, and Jimmy comes back to the car to open the door for us.

"Looks like we're all set." Dad rubs his belly. "I can taste the garlic from here."

Suit Man opens the door for us, and we walk through a very busy kitchen. Pots and pans clang, until the workers look up and see us. The clanging gets quieter. A few stare, but nobody says anything. Suit Man leads us into a small, back room with just a few tables, and motions to one of them. I can hear the hustle and bustle of people talking and plates clanking from the next room, but I can't see anyone else. As promised, we're alone.

A waitress comes in with water and menus.

"I think we know what we'd like," Dad says to the waitress, who smiles politely but looks at him with googly eyes. Even people who aren't baseball fans recognize Dad, since he's always in lots of magazines, and he's even a spokesperson for a really popular men's cologne that smells like a combination of fresh air and Astroturf. "Bea?"

"I'd like the ravioli, please."

"And I'll have the caprese salad," Mom says.

"The cavatelli and broccoli for me." Dad hands the waitress our menus, then adds, "With extra garlic."

After we place our order, the subject turns to school, which of course I knew it would. This is my chance. My big moment to tell them what I want for my birthday.

"Actually," I begin. "School hasn't been great."

"Oh no, honey." Mom furrows her eyebrows. "I thought things were going well."

"They were," I say. "And then they weren't."

"What happened?" Her eyebrows are practically touching now.

"My friends just didn't turn out to be who I thought they were." It took me days to come up with that line, and I practiced it again and again. I don't want to give them too much information, but I want to make my point clear. I think that line says just enough without giving up too much. At least I hope so.

"So that brings me to my birthday present." I take a deep breath in. My parents are staring at me, and Mom's eyebrows are *still* furrowed.

"I'd like to go away to school." There. I said it. I exhale.

"What do you mean, away?" Mom asks.

"Like to a boarding school. In Maine."

"In *Maine*?" Dad asks. Now his eyebrows are furrowed too.

"Yes. It's called Midcoast Academy. And I'd like to go there."

"How did you hear about this place?" Mom asks.

My palms get sweaty. I knew this question was coming, and I'm prepared. I hold my head up high. "I did some research."

"Research?" Dad squints his eyes, which is what he does when he's confused.

"Yes." I hold my head up higher.

"You do know how far Maine is from California?" Mom asks.

"Yes, I do."

"Why would you want to be so far away, Bea?" Dad rolls up his sleeves, but he keeps looking at me through squinty eyes.

"It's not that I want to be far away," I say. "It's just that I want to go to this particular school." Although this isn't the entire truth, it sounds very convincing coming out of my mouth. Probably because I've also practiced this line a hundred times. So far, I've anticipated all of their questions.

"What is it about this school that you like so much?" Mom asks. The waitress comes into the room with dinner salads. We all stop talking while she puts them on the table.

"I want to broaden my horizons," I say, after the waitress leaves.

"Broaden your horizons?" Mom asks slowly.

"Yes. I've lived in California for my whole entire life. You and Dad are friends with celebrities, so I know a few celebrity kids, but I don't know any normal kids. And I know you think the kids I go to school with are normal kids, but they're not. Normal kids don't get dropped off at school in limos. Normal kids aren't obsessed with being famous."

"You think your friends at school are like that?" Mom asks.

"I know they are." I swallow the lump forming in my throat.

"Well, Bea," Dad says in between bites of salad. "This is a pretty big decision. I think your mom and I need some more time to think about it."

"But today's my birthday. It's all I want for a present."

"I know, hon," Mom says. "But this isn't a decision we can make in one night. We need to check out the school, learn more. Maybe we can all go visit over the summer and you can start next year—"

"I don't want to start next year." I blink back tears. "I want to start now."

"Why all of a sudden?" Mom asks.

"It's not all of a sudden." I twist my napkin around my fingers. "I've been thinking about it for a while now. It's just that you haven't been here to talk about it."

"We'd hardly ever see you." Mom squeezes my hand.

"We'd still FaceTime. That's what we do now anyway."

I try not to play the guilt card too often, but tonight I have to put it on the table. I know my parents feel guilty that they're not around as much as they'd like. As I look at their faces, I know I got them. They feel bad.

I'm just not sure if they feel bad enough.

The waitress comes with our main course. Even though

my stomach is jumpy, I practically inhale my ravioli. It is *that* good.

"I know this isn't the present you really want." Dad hands me a small box, gift-wrapped in shiny orange wrapping paper. "But we hope you like it."

I unwrap the box, open it up, and find a silver chain with a shiny ruby dangling from it. "Thank you," I say. "I love it." And I really do. I almost feel bad for trying to guilt my parents into letting me go to boarding school.

Almost.

I decide not to say anything more about school until we get home. I don't want them to think I don't appreciate their gift.

After scarfing down a double-chocolate-mousse cake, we pay the check, and Suit Man escorts us out of the room. He opens the back door, and we head back to the parking lot, where we are met with a sudden bombardment of cameras and flashes.

Dad puts his arm around my shoulder and shields my face with his jacket. There are paparazzi everywhere. Jimmy is trying to drive the car toward us, but photographers just jump right in front of him. I wonder if it's illegal to run them over.

One of the photographers steps right in front of me, and Dad shoves him so hard that he falls. I stumble over him and wind up on my butt. Dad pulls me up and out of the way of the others, who seem to be multiplying. The bright lights are blinding me, and everyone's yelling at once—including Mom, who's using some very rude words. Jimmy finally reaches us and stops the car. He jumps out of the driver's seat and opens the back door. He grabs Mom's arm and ushers her in. I put my hands over my ears and squeeze my eyes shut as Dad pulls me into the car and slams the door.

The second the door closes, Jimmy peels out of the parking lot onto La Cienega Boulevard.

"Are you okay, Bea?" Dad asks.

"Yeah," I say. I look down at my beautiful silver dress, which is covered in dirt. At least it's not ripped. I'm sure I can get the dirt out. A rip would have been much harder to fix.

"I'm sorry, Mr. Miller," Jimmy says. "They appeared out of nowhere."

"That's okay, Jimmy," Dad says. "They always do."

"We were so careful." Mom throws her hands up in the air. "What is wrong with these people? Why can't they let anyone enjoy a family night out?"

"They're pariahs," Dad says, "but they're just doing their jobs."

"Maybe, but I don't know how they sleep at night." Mom's face is flushed.

I bite the inside of my cheek. "This is why I want to go to Maine." I'm surprised by how quietly this comes out.

Mom and Dad just look at me.

"This isn't normal," I say.

Now Mom and Dad look at each other. I swear they have some secret mind-reading thing going on. Mom sighs, and Dad nods. It's not an actual conversation, but I know they're thinking the same thing.

"Okay, hon," Mom says. "We'll look into this Midcoast Academy. No promises, though. We need to learn much more about it."

I lean over and give Mom a giant hug. I immediately know, deep down in my heart, that they'll let me go. I try to hide my beaming smile as I think about the fact that I will soon be away from Sophie and Damon and Hollywood and paparazzi. I will soon be a student of Midcoast Academy.

I will soon be normal.

# Chapter

## ★ 4 ★

I GO TO SCHOOL THE NEXT DAY BUT FAKE FEELING sick, hoping everyone will leave me alone. It doesn't work.

"How was Sarriette's?" Sophie asks during lunch.

"How'd you know I was at Sarriette's?" I pull the lid off my bowl of fruit salad.

"There were pictures online. Your dad's arm was blocking most of your face, but of course I knew it was you."

At least my face wasn't showing. My parents hate it when my picture gets out.

"So your parents are home?" Sophie pops a piece of pineapple into her mouth.

"Yeah, till Friday."

"Maybe I can come over after school this week. We can hang out." I stare at her. My blood boils as I look at her fake smile and her fake fingernails and the fake BFF necklace that I gave her for Christmas. I want to tell her that I know. I want to tell her that she isn't fooling me. I want to tell her that she's evil and rotten and mean. I want to tell her, but I don't. I do, however, notice that she's got lettuce in her teeth. I don't tell her that, either, and knowing that she's walking around with green teeth calms me down a little.

Somehow I make it through the rest of the day, and my parents are both on the deck when I get home.

"How was school, Bea?" Dad asks. He's standing over a pitcher of iced tea and pours me a glass.

"Not great." I take a sip. "Did you get a chance to look at the Midcoast Academy website?"

"Yes," Mom answers. "And while it looks lovely, you can't tell everything from a website. I think we need to visit. Maybe we can do that next month when Dad and I are home for a few weeks and—"

"I can't wait another month," I interrupt her.

"It's just a month, hon." Mom takes my hand.

"That's another month I'd have to spend at school." Tears fill my eyes, and no matter how hard I try to suck them back into my head, it's no use. They spill out.

"Oh, hon." Mom stands up and pulls me into a hug. "What is going on at school?"

I have no choice. If I never want to step foot in that school again, I know I've got to talk. In between sobs, I tell them everything. I tell them about Sophie and Damon and how they think I'm lame and boring and ugly.

"Bea." Dad takes my shoulders. "Those kids are just insecure and mean. I hope you don't believe what they said."

I don't know what I believe. All I know is that the thought of going back to that school and seeing Sophie's awful face makes my insides feel all twisted up.

"You are a beautiful girl, inside and out." Dad smiles and his eyes crinkle. "Your real friends will see that."

"That's just it," I say. "I don't have real friends here. That's why I want to try something new."

"I know, hon, but we won't have time to get to Maine before Dad and I have to get back on the road," Mom says.

"Can't Ellie go with me?" I know my parents have total trust in Ellie.

Mom and Dad look at each other, and I can tell they're having another one of their psychic conversations.

"I suppose she could," Mom says. "But we need to ask her."

I break out in a smile and fling open the French doors leading into the house. "Ellie! Ellie!" I run into the kitchen and find her sitting at the desk in front of the computer. "Can you come onto the deck? We want to ask you something."

"What is it, Bea?" Ellie asks as I grab her by the hand and pull her outside.

Mom and Dad are both standing now, talking to each other quietly.

"What is it, Bea?" Ellie asks again, pieces of her gray hair falling out of her bun.

"Well," Mom begins. "It seems Ruby is interested in attending a boarding school in Maine."

"Maine?" Ellie asks. "So far away, Bea?"

"I want to experience new things," I say in my most grown-up voice.

"I see," Ellie says, smoothing her bun with her hands.

"Ellie, would it be too much to ask of you to visit the school with Ruby? Zack has three games on the road, and I'm in the middle of a ten-city audition tour for the show. Ruby is very anxious to learn more about this place." Mom is talking to Ellie but looking at me, her eyebrows furrowed yet again.

"Of course, Ms. Celestine," Ellie says. "Of course I will go with her."

I jump up and down and throw my arms around Ellie. "Thank you! Thank you!"

"Can you ask Kathy to make the call and set up the visit?" Mom asks Ellie.

Ellie jots something down in a notebook she pulls out of her pocket and goes back inside. Mom and Dad are staring at me.

"Are you sure this is what you want, Bea?" Dad asks.

"I'm sure." I nod so hard I think my head might fall off.

"Okay," Dad says. "But if you like it, and if Ellie gives

us the thumbs-up, there will be some rules you'll have to follow."

"Anything," I say.

"You'll have to keep up with your grades," Mom says. "And FaceTime us every night, same as now."

"Of course," I say. "Of course I will."

"And one more thing." Dad's lips form a straight, thin line. "Don't come home talking funny. Remember to say your *r*'s."

I stare at him blankly, and he cracks up. I laugh too, even though I have no idea why.

Ellie opens the door to the deck and steps outside, notebook in hand. "We're all set, Bea. We leave tomorrow afternoon, and we'll tour the school on Friday."

I bounce up and down for at least a minute, hug my parents, then Ellie, then my parents again—then fly upstairs to my room to pack.

# Chapter
## ⋆ 5 ⋆

𝒥IMMY BRINGS US TO THE AIRPORT. MOM AND DAD join us for the ride, and we have a family good-bye hug on the sidewalk outside the terminal. It has to be quick before someone recognizes us.

There are no tears. This is normal for my family. A series of comings and goings. Even when I used to go on the road with them, we didn't spend much time together. They were busy, and I hung out with Ellie. They probably would have rathered Ellie and I stayed home, but I insisted on going with them. It wasn't until I started middle school that I decided I wanted to go to school instead of being tutored on the road.

Ellie and I board our plane and settle into our first-class seats. Ellie orders a glass of wine the minute we sit down, like she does every time we fly. I must have fallen asleep immediately, because the next thing I realize, I'm waking up to the sound of the captain's voice.

"We have begun our initial descent into the Portland area, and will be arriving at the Portland International Jetport in approximately twenty minutes. Please make sure your seat belts are fastened, your seats are in their upright position, and your tray tables are secured. It's been a pleasure having you on board today. Thank you for flying with us."

"That was fast," I say through a yawn.

"For you, maybe." Ellie's hands are gripping the seat rests. Even though she flies with us all the time, she hates it.

I laugh. "Relax, Ellie. We're almost there."

"I will relax when we are on the ground, like human beings belong." She squeezes her eyes shut.

I stretch and look out the window. It's dark, but I can see that we're getting close to landing. I hear a few dings, and Ellie grabs my hand. Her fingernails are digging into my skin, but I don't say anything. She's doing me a huge favor by taking me here, and I don't want her to feel bad—even though she's leaving crescent-shaped dents in my hand. She loosens her grip when we land and breathes a big sigh of relief as we taxi down the runway.

We're the first ones off the plane, and it's a short walk to the baggage area. There's a driver holding a sign with Ellie's name on it. We always use Ellie's name when we travel because we can't ever use ours. As if it would matter.

My parents are instantly recognizable, even without a sign.

The driver helps us with our bags and takes us to his car, a stretch limo.

I groan.

"Please tell me we're not going to take this to the school tomorrow."

"You don't like it, Bea? Such a beautiful car."

"It's not that." I bite the inside of my cheek. "I just don't think that most of the kids who go to Midcoast Academy ride in limos."

"Mmmm." Ellie nods her head. "I see."

"I just don't want to seem too weird."

Ellie's still nodding. Even though she doesn't say anything I feel like I should keep talking.

"It's not like at home, Ellie. These kids are normal. Normal kids don't ride to school in limos."

"You want to be normal, Bea?"

I look down at my hands. "Sometimes."

"Mmmm." Ellie nods again. "But remember to be proud of who you are."

As much as I love Ellie, she doesn't understand. I've grown up hearing the stories of her childhood in Russia. She grew up poor, with eight brothers and sisters in a tiny house. Her mother died when she was five years old, and her father was really mean. She's always telling me how lucky I am to have parents who love me and can afford to give me nice things.

The car ride is taking forever. I'm not sure if I can't sleep because I slept on the plane or because it feels like there are a million butterflies in my stomach. I stare out the window, amazed that I see nothing but darkness. No streetlights, no cities. I don't even see any other cars on the road.

I'm definitely not in Los Angeles anymore.

The car slows down and pulls into the driveway of what looks like a gigantic house.

"Did we rent a house?" I squint out the window.

"This is a bed-and-breakfast," Ellie explains. "Only a few blocks from the school."

"You mean we could walk there?" I practically squeal since that means I won't have to show up in a stretch limo.

"I suppose so. Let us see what the weather is like tomorrow."

I'm not sure what the big deal is until I get out of the car. The wind cuts through my jacket and bites my skin. Nope. This is definitely *not* LA.

Ellie checks us into the bed-and-breakfast, which is toasty warm thanks to a big stone fireplace in the middle of the house.

A woman with short gray hair takes us up to our rooms.

"So you're here to look at Midcoast Academy?" she says,

even though it sounds like she says *So you a heeya to look at Midcoast Academy?*

"Yes," I answer politely. "We're going to tour the school tomorrow."

"Well isn't that nice." She pulls a key off a giant key ring and unlocks the door. "The school is wonderful." Which sounds like *wondah-full.*

My room is attached to Ellie's, with a bathroom in between. Ellie's room is decorated in moose paraphernalia. There's a lamp with a moose base, framed pictures of moose on the wall, and a red bedspread with moose in different poses. My room is a sea theme, with pictures of lobsters, starfish, and sailboats lining the walls.

I glance at the clock on the wall, which has lighthouses where the numbers should be. It's almost midnight, and we have to be at school at eight thirty. I yawn. After a quick shower, I pull on the warmest nightgown I own, white flannel with pink tulips, and crawl into bed.

The next thing I know, Ellie is knocking on my door.

"Bea, time to get up, sweetheart."

I open my eyes, barely, blinking until I get used to the light.

"Okay, okay. I'm up." I throw the blankets off me and stretch my arms above my head. I manage to get myself into a seated position and rub my eyes.

"You have half an hour to get ready," Ellie says.

I drag myself out of bed and shuffle to the bathroom. My

hair's way too curly and crazy for a comb, so I add some gel and fluff it up with my fingers. I have no idea what kids wear at Midcoast Academy, so I play it safe with a pair of jeans and a bright orange hoodie with shiny silver zippers up the sleeves. The jeans show that I'm approachable, while the hoodie makes the look uniquely "me." I add the ruby necklace my parents gave me, then brush my lips with the strawberry lip gloss that Sophie got me for my birthday. Even though Sophie's a horrible friend, at least she has excellent taste in lip gloss.

Ellie and I find breakfast waiting for us in the formal dining room. My stomach gets more gurgly by the minute, but I manage to stuff my face with the most mouthwatering blueberry pancakes I've ever tasted.

Thank goodness Ellie decides the weather's decent enough to walk to the school. The air is super cold, but the sky is bright blue and sunny.

"Button up your coat," Ellie says as we step onto the sidewalk. "It's cold here in Maine."

I breathe in deeply. When I let it out, I can see my breath. "I think it's refreshing."

Ellie chuckles. "You have a young person's bones."

We follow the sidewalk as it passes by Victorian houses with giant front porches. Most of the trees are still bare, but there are *tons* of them. I recognize the pines and oaks and maples from my science class. Huge evergreens line the yards. I take a deep breath—it smells like Christmas—and there's not a palm tree in sight.

Soon the houses disappear and are replaced by little shops. We pass a chocolate store, a coffee shop, a bookstore, too many restaurants to count, and about three ice cream places. I'm in love already.

And just when I think things couldn't get any better, we turn the corner and find ourselves in front of a quaint park overlooking a marina crowded with boats of all shapes and sizes. The water beyond glimmers like diamonds. Sure, we have tons of marinas in Southern California, but this is different somehow—like an old-fashioned painting. There's nothing old-fashioned back home.

The wind whips at my hair so it stands straight up, and I pull my hood onto my head. Ellie is wearing a wool hat, scarf, and gloves, and she's still complaining about the cold. I think Ellie's been in Southern California too long.

I see the sign before she does. The gold letters glisten in the sunlight. MIDCOAST ACADEMY.

"We're here, Ellie, we're here!" I jump up and down and pull her arm so she'll walk faster.

I practically skip down the sidewalk as Ellie shuffles along behind me. The campus is made up of what looks like a bunch of big houses with winding pathways between them. Kids with backpacks stroll along the pathways, talking and laughing. I spot a building that says MAIN OFFICE above the door. I glance back at Ellie, and she nods for me to go inside.

A tall lady with bright red hair peeks up from behind a desk in an office to our right and stands when she sees us.

"Hello." She walks over and extends her hand, which I shake politely. "You must be Ruby."

"Hello," I say.

"I'm Mrs. Kearney," she says. "I'm the admissions director here at Midcoast."

I think it's funny that Mrs. Kearney is dressed in a fancy business suit, but she has purple duck boots on her feet. Nobody in Hollywood wears purple duck boots, and I decide right then and there that I must get a pair.

"Come sit down." She ushers us into the office she just came out of and closes the door behind her. "Can I get you some coffee, tea?"

I almost agree to coffee when I notice she's looking at Ellie and not me. I wonder if kids around here don't drink coffee.

"How about you, Ruby? Would you like some water, or hot chocolate?"

There's my answer.

"No thank you," I say, deciding not to ask for coffee.

There's a knock on the office door, and Mrs. Kearney opens it.

"Hello, Summer. You're right on time." She turns to me.

"Ruby, this is Summer. Summer, this is Ruby. Summer will be showing you around today."

"Oh, that is so nice, Bea," Ellie says. "A student will give you the tour."

"Yes, I think Summer will be much more interesting than me." Mrs. Kearney laughs and then turns to Summer. "Go ahead and get started. We'll catch up."

Ellie and Mrs. Kearney talk, and Summer opens the door for me. I follow her out of the office and back into the entryway. She totally looks like a Summer. Her windblown hair is dirty blond with lighter blond streaks, and she has a splash of freckles across her nose. She's wearing a pink skirt over purple tights with yellow polka dots, and on top of those she's wearing knee-high socks that don't match. A pair of flowered rubber boots cover her feet. I could never wear something like that, but she pulls the look off perfectly.

"Is your name Ruby or Bea? 'Cause Mrs. Kearney said Ruby, but your mom said Bea."

"Oh, that's not my mom," I say.

"Who is she, then?" Summer asks.

"My nanny," I say.

Summer blinks but doesn't say anything. My face heats up. What if normal kids don't have nannies? Did I just blow it with her, talking about my nanny? I have to fix this immediately.

"I mean my nana. She's my nana." The words spill out of my mouth.

"Oh, I have a nana too. She lives in New Jersey."

I exhale.

"So how come your nana brought you and not your parents?"

"My parents couldn't bring me," I say. My palms are getting sweaty, and I wipe them on my jeans.

"How come?" she asks.

I wasn't expecting this question. I can't tell her the truth, that my mom's the host of the number-one-rated TV show *America's Next Cover Model* and my dad's the most popular player in the major leagues, and by the way, did I mention that my mom is Celestine Cruz and my dad is Zack Miller and the only reason you'll want to be friends with me is to meet them?

"I don't have parents." I have no idea why I say that. This conversation is happening too fast.

"What happened to them?"

"They died."

*What am I doing?* Why was that the first thing that popped into my head? Lines of sweat are dripping down the back of my neck, and I feel like my face will melt off any second.

"Oh." Summer looks me right in the eyes. "I'm really sorry. I hope you're okay."

"I'm—fine," I stammer. "It was—it was a long time ago. I barely remember when it happened." Which is probably because it never did happen.

She nods. "Well, I think you'll really like it here."

"You do?" I ask, grateful that we're done talking about my parents, who apparently I don't have.

"Oh yeah. The kids are a lot of fun, and the teachers are really nice. I mean, math is still math and it's still really boring, but art and PE and drama are awesome."

Summer leads me outside, and we walk on a path that winds between buildings. "So should I call you Ruby or Bea?"

I've never thought about that before. Only my family calls me Bea. But this is a new place. New friends. And now, I decide, a new name.

"My full name is Ruby, but I like to be known as Bea."

"Okay, Bea." Summer gives me a smile. "What do you want to see first?"

# Chapter
## ★ 6 ★

MIDCOAST ACADEMY IS AMAZING.

Summer shows me the middle school classrooms, the gym, the theater, the art room, the garden, and the soccer fields. We meet some of her friends, and everyone is super sweet. Ellie and Mrs. Kearney are following us, but they're busy talking with each other.

"Summer," Mrs. Kearney calls. "Why don't you take Ruby to the dorms and show her around?"

"Sure, Mrs. Kearney," Summer says. "But she wants to be called Bea."

"Okay then." Mrs. Kearney smiles. "Take Bea to the dorms and show her around."

I glance back at Ellie. She looks at me, eyebrows raised, but I see that her lips are curling into a small smile.

I follow Summer into a bigger building. This one doesn't look anything like the others we visited. It's more like a motel, complete with a lobby and a couple of vending machines.

Summer swipes a card next to a glass door and pulls it open. I follow her, and the door clicks shut behind us. We step into a long hallway with doors on each side, just like in those motels you find off the highway. I went to one once when my mom's manager booked her in the wrong place. I follow Summer up a flight of stairs, and then down another long hallway.

"So everyone who goes to the school lives here?" I look around at all the doors, each one decorated differently.

"Not everyone." Summer bounces down the hall, which is pretty quiet since kids are in class. "But a lot of us. This is the middle school dorm. The girls are in one wing and the boys are in another. The high school dorm is in another building."

Summer stops at a door with a hot pink corkboard. There are Post-it notes tacked all over it, some with pictures of smiley faces, some with just writing. Summer puts her key in the lock and pushes the door open. Half of the room is an explosion of hot pink. There's a hot pink fuzzy rug, a hot pink beanbag chair, and a hot pink bedspread. Another hot pink corkboard hangs from the wall above the bed, this one ten times bigger than the one hanging on the door. It's covered with postcards and photos. Posters of puppies and kittens hang on either side of the window, which faces out into a courtyard.

"This is my room. And your room, if you decide to go here."

"Really?" I can't help but smile. "We'd be roommates?"

"Yep." Summer kicks her boots off and bounces on her bed. "I had a roommate last semester but she left. She was really homesick. Want to jump?"

"On your bed?" I eyeball the twin bed and wonder if it would fit both of us.

"No, on your bed!" Summer laughs.

I glance over at the empty bed on the other side of the room. I carefully take my shoes off, put them by the side of the door. I climb onto the bed and lightly jump up and down.

Summer cracks up. "That's not jumping. Your feet are barely moving."

I bounce a little harder and go a little higher. A giggle escapes my lips, and within seconds I'm laughing harder than I've laughed in months.

"Your hair looks so crazy right now!" Summer says. "It's standing straight up."

"So is yours!" I laugh even harder when I try to picture Sophie jumping on a bed. As if Sophie would ever do *any-thing* to mess up her hair.

Summer stops jumping and flops down on the bed.

"That was fun. I guess we should keep going, though, or Mrs. Kearney will think we got lost or something."

We head back downstairs, but instead of going out the main door, we go out a different one that leads into the court-yard I saw out Summer's window. Tables and chairs cover a stone patio, and benches sit underneath tall oak trees.

As we're about to go back to the main campus, a bunch of kids come pouring outside. They're led by a man with shaggy brown hair and a short beard. The man waves us over.

"Summer, why don't you introduce us to your new friend?"

"Sure, Mr. Desmond." Summer takes me by the hand, and we take a few steps toward the group.

"This is Bea. She's visiting Midcoast today." Summer then motions to the man. "This is Mr. Desmond, my science teacher. And these are the kids in my class."

Everyone talks at once. They're all smiling and welcoming me. Some even shake my hand.

"Okay, okay," Mr. Desmond says. "Let's give Bea some breathing room."

I look down at the ground and smile. It feels weird to have everyone staring at me, but not bad weird like when I'm out with my parents.

"Well, Bea." Mr. Desmond smiles at me. "I hope you're enjoying your tour, and maybe we'll see you here soon."

"Yes, thank you. I hope so." I'm still looking at the ground.

"Summer, we'll see you when you get back to class," Mr. Desmond says to her.

"Okeydokey," Summer says. "See you then."

Some of the kids say stuff to her as they walk by. I notice a boy stops to talk to her for a longer time. She's whispering to him, and he's nodding, his light brown hair falling into his eyes. He smiles, and I notice that he has huge dimples just like Damon Gorman. My stomach flip-flops a little.

Nice teachers, a totally fun roommate, three ice cream shops nearby, a place where nobody knows who my parents are, *and* cute boys?

I must sign up immediately.

# Chapter
## ★ 7 ★

MOM'S AND DAD'S FACES APPEAR ON MY IPAD.

"So, tell us all about it." Mom's grinning. A good sign.

I tell them about Summer and the campus and the dorms. They smile and nod, but I don't get the green light yet.

"Why don't you let us talk to Ellie?" Mom says.

The bathroom door that separates our rooms is open, and I can see that Ellie is going through her suitcase.

"Ellie!" Mom and Dad both cringe a little when I yell. "Can you come in here?"

Ellie stands behind me at the desk. I get up and let her sit in the chair so Mom and Dad can see her. Before I move behind her, I give her a pleading look with my eyes, praying she understands. I cross my fingers behind my back for extra luck.

"Hi, Ellie," Dad says. "How's Maine?"

"It is cold." Ellie pulls her sweater tighter. "But maybe not as cold as Siberia."

Dad laughs. "What did you think of the school?"

I cross another set of fingers.

"It was very nice, Mr. Zack."

"I did a little more research," Mom says. "It seems Midcoast Academy has an excellent academic reputation. Everything I've read about it sounds great, but sometimes research doesn't tell the whole story. Did you get a good vibe, Ellie? I really hate being so far away for a decision like this."

"Oh yes, Ms. Celestine. Everyone was very nice and Bea liked the other students. Mrs. Kearney told me that they have an immediate opening and Bea can begin once the papers are signed."

"So it has the Ellie stamp of approval?"

I hold my breath.

"Yes, I approve." She wraps her arms around herself. "But brrrr—it is cold! Reminds me of Russia."

I exhale and do a little dance behind Ellie. My smile is so wide that I think it may push my ears behind my head. I switch places with Ellie so my parents can see my face.

"Thank you, thank you, thank you," I say, bouncing up and down in the chair.

"Wait a minute, hon." Mom holds her hand up in front of her face. "I still need to talk to Mrs. Kearney myself."

"Of course." I tilt my head and put on my most grown-up expression. "But wouldn't it be best for me to just stay and start on Monday, instead of flying back and forth? I don't want to miss any more classes than I have to, and I could have my stuff sent here."

Mom purses her lips. "It's not ideal that Dad and I can't see the place for ourselves, but I can see the sense in you staying. We really don't want you to miss any more school than necessary either. How about I contact Mrs. Kearney first thing tomorrow morning."

I fist-pump the air. I know my mom will love Mrs. Kearney.

"Remember our deal." Mom's face gets serious. "Good grades and FaceTime every night."

"Yes, I remember." I nod my head up and down.

"We'll miss you when we're home next month, Bea," Dad says, looking sad.

"I'll miss you, too, but I'll be home in less than three months for summer."

"Maybe we can find a time to come visit before then." Dad's face lights up.

"Yes, maybe during that break we have in May," Mom adds.

I bite the inside of my cheek. There's no way my parents can visit Midcoast. I don't want anyone to know who they are. Oh, and there's the small problem that I told Summer I was an *orphan.*

"Okay." I push the thought out of my mind. "Let's talk about it as we get closer." Maybe something will come up, and they won't be able to make it anyway. Something always comes up with my parents' crazy schedules. If there's one thing I can count on with my family, it's that nothing is ever the way it's supposed to be.

For once, I'm happy about that.

# Chapter
## ★ 8 ★

IT'S DECORATING DAY.

We decide to pick up some linens and decorations for my side of the room I'll share with Summer. At breakfast Ellie asks the lady who runs the bed-and-breakfast where the nearest mall is. When she tells us that it's over an hour away, I almost spit out my orange juice. An hour to the nearest mall? In LA there are malls every five blocks.

"What are you looking for?" the lady asks as she pours Ellie's coffee. I breathe the scent of the coffee in, then sigh. I *have* to kick the coffee habit now that I'm with normal kids.

"Bed linens, things for Bea's new room," Ellie says.

"Oh, there's a wonderful store that carries those things right in town," the lady says, adding that we could walk there. Which puts a big fat smile on my face. I would just die if Summer or that boy with the dimples saw me tooling around town in a limo.

On Monday Ellie and I go back to Midcoast to officially register. Luckily, the paperwork is all ready because Mom and Dad signed everything over e-mail.

"Welcome to Midcoast." Mrs. Kearney smiles when the registration is complete. "I had a lovely conversation with your parents this morning. I understand your things are being shipped and should arrive by the end of the week."

"Yes," Ellie says. "Bea and I did some shopping over the weekend so we have all she will need until then." She motions toward three huge shopping bags filled with bed linens, window curtains, towels, and other cute decorations I picked up on our shopping spree. Ellie tried to convince me to take the limo to school so we wouldn't have to walk while carrying all of our bags, plus my suitcase, but I begged her to let us walk, and even offered to carry everything myself. She finally gave in, and actually carried two of the bags herself.

"Great." Mrs. Kearney picks up one of the bags. "I'll take you up to the dorms so you can get settled in."

Mrs. Kearney gives me a card and shows me how to swipe it so the glass door that leads from the lobby to the dorm rooms opens. We take the staircase to the second floor.

"There's a teacher living on each floor, so we always have a member of the faculty nearby." We follow Mrs. Kearney down the hall toward Summer's—and my—room. "Your floor parent is Ms. Goldberg. She's the art teacher. The girls here love her."

Mrs. Kearney stops at a door marked RESTROOMS. "This is the bathroom." She opens the door, and we peek our heads in. "There are six sinks, six bathroom stalls, and four showers in the back. First come, first served for the showers."

I've never shared a bathroom before. With anyone. At least it's clean. Mrs. Kearney closes the door, and we continue down the hall.

When we get to the door with the hot pink corkboard, Mrs. Kearney gives a quick knock. I'm not sure why. The dorms are empty since everyone's in class. She then puts a key in the lock, and the door to my new life opens.

"Oh, Bea, this is such a lovely room." Ellie puts the bag she's carrying on the floor next to my bed.

It is. It *is* a lovely room. In fact, it's the best room ever because I'm going to share it with Summer and it's 3,174 miles away from Hollywood and Sophie and Damon and the paparazzi. Mrs. Kearney tells us to stop back in her office when we're done unpacking.

Ellie and I start by putting the sheets on the bed. The comforter I picked out is orange and hot pink. I hope Summer likes it.

After the posters are hung and the towels are put away on a shelf in my closet, Ellie pulls a heavy-looking box from the corner of the room and slides it over to me.

"Where did this come from?" I study the box at my feet.

"I had it shipped to Mrs. Kearney's office. I asked her to bring it up here when you registered. Open it," she says, smiling.

I lift up the flaps and peer inside. Ellie's prized vintage Singer sewing machine peeks out at me.

"Oh, Ellie!" I gently lift the sewing machine out. It weighs a ton, but I hold on to it as if it's made of glass. "I can't take this."

"Don't be silly." Ellie waves her hand. "Of course you can."

"But it's your sewing machine. I know how much you love it."

"Meh." Ellie shrugs. "You use it more than I do. I want you to have it."

"Really, Ellie? You sure?" I hug the sewing machine to my chest like it's my long lost teddy bear.

"Yes, Bea."

"Thank you, Ellie, thank you!"

"Just promise me you will use it, eh? Promise you will keep making those beautiful clothes." Ellie looks me right in the eyes.

"I promise." And I really, truly mean it.

I put the sewing machine on the corner of my desk, then throw my arms around Ellie and squeeze.

"Let's go, bubela." Ellie releases me and turns toward

the door, her voice shaky. "You didn't come all the way here to sit in your room with an old lady."

I lock the dorm room door, and Ellie and I make our way back to Mrs. Kearney's office. Ellie's flight leaves this afternoon, and while I'm sure I'll miss her bunches, I can't wait to start my new life here.

"You're just in time for lunch, Bea," Mrs. Kearney says when she sees us. "I'll take you over to the cafeteria when you're ready."

I walk Ellie to the main office, and out onto the front lawn. The limo's parked just down the road, and I look around to be sure nobody's watching. When I'm sure we're alone, I give her another giant hug.

"I'm going to miss you, Ellie." I feel tears bubbling up, and I squeeze my eyes tight shut to keep them from flowing out.

"Oh, Bea." Ellie kisses my forehead. "I will miss you so very much."

We stand there hugging for a few more seconds, and then she takes my shoulders and looks right in my eyes.

"Bea, you are a beautiful person. You just be yourself and you will be very happy here."

I nod and wipe a tear away with the back of my hand. Ellie hugs me again, and then shuffles off to the limo.

I blink a few times, take a deep breath, and reapply my lip gloss before going back to Mrs. Kearney's office, where she's waiting to take me to lunch. I know I should be hungry, but I can't help feeling a little sad. Even though I'm exactly where I want to be, it was hard to see Ellie go. Harder even than leaving my parents. Ellie's been with me forever, and suddenly my stomach feels empty, and not because it's lunchtime.

I follow Mrs. Kearney to the cafeteria. It actually smells pretty good, and as we get closer, my stomach growls a little. Summer spots us and waves me over.

"Hey!" She gives me a hug. "They told me you'd be starting today." Summer's wearing black leggings under a pink polka-dotted skirt. Her striped sweater has every color in the rainbow on it *except* pink. And, just like on Friday, her socks don't match.

"I hope you don't mind," I say. "I decorated my side of the room a little."

"That's super awesome." Summer pulls me to the end of the cafeteria line. "I was sick of looking at a half-empty room."

I smile. Summer hands me a tray and picks a bean burrito for herself. The pizza looks especially cheesy, but since Summer's getting the burrito, I get the burrito too. I'm just about to get a soda, but Summer chooses water. I look around. Maybe kids here don't drink soda. Just in case, I get the water. At least Mom would be happy that I made a healthier choice.

I follow Summer to a circular table with six chairs. She takes one, and I take the seat next to her. Even before I can sit down, the most glamorous girl I've seen yet at Midcoast

Academy slams her tray on the table and sits down on the opposite side of Summer. She stretches her legs out onto the empty chair next to her, showing off skinny jeans that fall straight into a pair of black knee-high leather boots. The boots are expensive, but they don't say anything about the girl wearing them, except that she spent a lot of money.

"Can you believe Mrs. Turner? That assignment is the *worst*."

Summer shrugs. "It's not that bad."

"Are you kidding me," the girl says. "I'll never get it done on time." She looks like she's about to say something else when she notices me.

"Oh, hi." She flashes me a smile, but it's one of those closed-mouth smiles that don't show her teeth. She's wearing very shiny lip gloss, so it looks like her lips are glued together.

"Hi." I smile back.

"Cassandra, this is Bea. Bea, this is Cassandra." Summer takes a sip of water.

"Is this the new girl?" Cassandra asks Summer, as if I'm invisible or something.

Summer takes a huge bite of burrito and nods.

"Cool," Cassandra says. "You look familiar."

"I do?" I look down at my plate. My parents do a pretty good job of shielding me from the paparazzi, but every once in a while a photo sneaks out.

"Yeah, but you're from California, right?"

"Uh-huh," I say.

She squints her eyes and stares at me for a few seconds. I say a silent prayer that she doesn't read tabloids or look at celebrity gossip online. "It must have totally sucked for you to leave California to come here," she finally says.

"Nope. I was looking forward to a change of scenery." I keep looking down at my plate, carefully cutting my burrito with my plastic fork. I look over at Summer, who has just picked the whole thing up with her hands. I probably would have done that too, if Cassandra weren't staring at me.

"But it's totally boring here." Cassandra polishes her apple.

"Cassandra's from New York," Summer says in between bites of burrito.

"Oh, New York's awesome," I say.

"Yeah, but not as awesome as California." Cassandra leans forward in her chair. "Have you ever seen any famous people?"

I shove a forkful of burrito into my mouth before I can answer. Luckily, another girl approaches the table, so Cassandra seems to forget about her question.

"Hey, Katie." Cassandra takes her feet off the chair next to her.

"Hi, guys," the girl says. Unlike Cassandra, she notices me right away and smiles. "I'm Katie."

"Hi, Katie. I'm Bea." I'm afraid to smile back in case I have beans in my teeth.

"Nice to meet you. Summer told us you were coming."

"Oh. My. God." Cassandra's voice drops to a whisper. "How hot does Connor look with his new haircut?" She motions her head to two boys in the cafeteria line.

"He got his hair cut like three weeks ago." Summer laughs.

"No way. I would have noticed," Cassandra says.

"It's true. I went with him to the barber shop." Summer wipes her face with a napkin.

Her plate is totally clean, but I still have half a burrito left. It's really good, but I don't want to seem too piglike on my first day.

Cassandra crosses her arms and stares at Summer.

"What?" Summer asks.

"Are you sure you guys aren't, like, dating?"

Summer looks at Cassandra sideways and rolls her eyes.

"Well, you're always together," Cassandra says.

"They're best friends," Katie interjects.

"Yeah, yeah." Cassandra takes a bite of her apple. Amazingly, her lip gloss stays on.

Summer leans back in her chair and stretches her legs out.

"Seriously, Summer." Cassandra glances at Summer's feet. "Do you ever wear anything that matches?"

I don't mean to, but I think I gasp a little. I don't know Summer well enough to predict what she'll do. Will she get really mad at Cassandra? Will she start to cry? Maybe she'll storm off and leave me sitting here with these girls I don't even know.

But Summer doesn't do any of those things. She just laughs and says, "No."

Cassandra sighs. "You're so weird. Can't you put in a good word for me with Connor?"

"Sure, Cass," Summer says. "I'll try."

I'm shocked. They just go right back to their conversation, as if Cassandra never insulted Summer's socks or called her weird or *anything*.

"Shhhh." Cassandra leans her face in closer to the table. "He's coming over here." She tries to smooth her hair and sits up straight.

I look up and see the two boys from the cafeteria line heading our way. One of the boys is the cute dimpled boy I saw Summer talking to when she gave me the tour. I wonder if that's the one Cassandra's talking about. He's definitely the cuter of the two. I put my plastic fork down and wipe the corners of my mouth with my napkin. I pray my face isn't covered in bean juice.

There are only two seats left, one next to Katie and one next to me. Cute Dimple Boy puts his tray down next to mine and sits down. He smiles at me for a fraction of a second, then looks back at his tray. I'm pretty sure my face is on fire. I can't tell if it's because Cute Dimple Boy is sitting next to me, or if I used too much hot sauce on my burrito. I take a big gulp of ice water.

"Hey, guys." Cassandra flips her hair.

"What's up?" the other boy says.

"Bea, this is Connor and Shane." Summer points to me, then to them.

"What's up?" Shane nods his head toward me.

"Nice to meet you," Connor, the cute one, says. He looks at me for a fraction of a second. I swear I would have missed it if I blinked. He may have the Damon Gordon dimples, but he absolutely does not have the Damon Gordon stare. Which is just as well, since maybe he doesn't notice that my face is as red as Cassandra's apple.

"Hi." I smile in their general direction. I take another gulp of water, hoping my face returns to its normal color before Connor looks at me again. Which he doesn't. Instead, he's having a conversation with Cassandra. Or more like Cassandra's having a conversation with him.

"OMG, Connor. I can't believe you already finished that homework. It was practically impossible."

"It wasn't too bad." Connor takes a bite of his pizza. I should have gotten the pizza.

"Then maybe you can help me figure it out." I swear Cassandra is actually batting her eyelashes. I don't think I've ever seen anyone do that in real life.

Connor shrugs. "Maybe."

"Okay, when?" Cassandra takes out her phone.

"When what?" Connor takes another bite of pizza.

"When can you help me? After school?"

"I guess."

"Cool." Cassandra types something in her phone. "I'll see you in the library right after last period. Come on, Katie."

She struts away before Connor can say anything else, with Katie at her heels.

Shane elbows Connor in the side. "Dude, she's totally into you."

"Whatever," Connor says, then turns to Summer. "Clara's Café tomorrow night?"

"Of course. It's Tuesday."

"Awesome."

"Every Tuesday my parents take us out to Clara's Café for dinner," Summer explains.

"You see your parents every week?"

"Oh." Summer looks down at her empty plate. "That was totally rude of me. I shouldn't just talk about my parents like that—"

"Oh no," I interrupt. "No, it's fine." Ugh. She thinks she hurt my feelings because my parents pretend "died." My stomach sinks into my shoes.

"Summer told me. I'm really sorry," Connor says. His voice is so quiet that it takes me a second to realize he's talking to me.

"Oh, uhhh, it's okay," I say. "I mean, thanks."

"My parents died too." He's tearing pieces off the crust of his pizza.

"Oh gosh. Wow," I say. "That's awful."

"Yeah, well, I wanted to tell you that I know how you feel."

*How I feel?* I turn bright red and feel like my face is on fire. I try to take a deep breath in, but the air feels stuck in my throat, and I cough. Thankfully, Summer jumps into the conversation.

"I hope you don't mind that I told him, Bea. I thought it might be nice to know someone that understands."

"Oh yes. Yes, it is."

I pray that someone will pull the fire alarm. Or that a fight will break out. Or that a meteor will strike the cafeteria right now at this very second.

"Anyway," Summer says. "My parents take me and my sister out to dinner every Tuesday to this amazing restaurant called Clara's Café. Connor always comes. You're invited too."

"Really? Are you sure? I don't want to intrude." Which is true. But I *would* like to have dinner with Summer and Connor.

"My parents would love to have you. They're cool like that."

"They totally are." Connor leans back in his chair. "They're like my pseudo parents."

"If you're sure, I'd really like to go."

"Great!" Summer stands up and grabs her tray. "Do you have your schedule?"

I open up my backpack and peek inside. "I have technology next."

"So do we," Summer says. I pick up my tray, which still has half a burrito left, and follow Summer and Connor to the back of the cafeteria.

"You can throw the rest of your burrito in the compost." Summer points to a big bin with a cover on top.

"The what?" I stare at the bin.

"The compost. It's where most of the food scraps go. It then gets turned into soil for the garden, which we use to grow our own veggies."

"The school grows its own food?"

Summer giggles. "This place must be really different from home."

I smile. That's the understatement of the year.

# Chapter

## ★ 9 ★

ALL MY AFTERNOON CLASSES ARE WITH SUMMER, which is fantastic. She makes sure I'm where I'm supposed to be at the right time. And she introduces me to everybody in our class so I don't just sit there like a loser.

Connor only has technology and science with us, but Cassandra is in every one of our classes.

"Did it bother you, what Cassandra said?" I ask Summer when we're back in our room after dinner.

Summer laughs. "Which time? Cassandra does a *lot* of talking." Summer sits cross-legged on her bed.

"When she said that thing about you not matching."

"Naaaah. She's right. I don't match."

"But she called you weird."

"That's because I am."

I blink.

Summer gets up and starts jumping on the bed. "I am weird. But I like myself that way."

I watch Summer bounce up and down. She's jumping so high I'm afraid her head will hit the ceiling. There's a knock on the door, and Summer yells, "Come in!"

The door opens, and a lady peeks her head in. She sees Summer and smiles for just a second before her face gets all serious looking.

"Summer, please don't jump on the bed." The lady pushes the door open all the way and walks in.

"Sorry, Ms. Goldberg." Summer does one more bounce when Ms. Goldberg turns away, and then sits down.

"You must be Bea." Ms. Goldberg sticks out her hand, which I politely shake. "It's so nice to meet you. I'm Liz Goldberg. I'm the floor parent here."

I remember Mrs. Kearney saying something about a Ms. Goldberg.

"Has Summer gone over the rules with you?" she asks.

"Rule number one," Summer says. "No jumping on the bed." She runs over to Ms. Goldberg and gives her a big hug.

"Very funny." Ms. Goldberg hugs her back. "But it is true that you're not supposed to jump on the bed." Ms. Goldberg raises one eyebrow and looks at Summer, who smiles.

"And," Ms. Goldberg continues, "we try to keep the noise down when we're here in our rooms. No hot plates, toasters, or microwave ovens allowed. No boys allowed. And lights out is at nine o'clock, but it's okay to keep a reading light on by your bed if you'd like. I think those are the biggies."

"Okay," I say.

"And of course, I'm always here if you need an adult to talk to."

I nod.

"Well, Bea, welcome. I look forward to getting to know you."

"Thank you, Ms. Goldberg."

"And Summer, keep the bouncing to a minimum, okay?"

"Yep." Summer smiles and flops down on her bed.

"I'll be back for lights out, in about an hour." Ms. Goldberg closes the door behind her.

"Wow, it's eight o'clock already." Summer groans. "I still have to shower."

Oh no. Eight o'clock. FaceTime.

I glance at my iPad, which is open on my desk. Mom always calls me, so it's going to ring any minute now, and Zack Miller and Celestine Cruz are going to pop up on my screen and Summer's going to see and wonder why on earth Zack Miller and Celestine Cruz are calling me because after all Zack Miller and Celestine Cruz are hugely famous and supposed normal people like me don't know celebrities like them.

I suck in a big breath of air and squeeze my eyes real

tight. I try to think of a way to FaceTime my parents without Summer noticing. Oh no, oh no, oh no. I hadn't thought about this at all. Even if I manage to hide my screen she'll know I'm talking to somebody. And since my headphones aren't here yet she'll hear them and know they're parent-like. Oh no, oh no, oh no.

Summer hops up off the bed. "I'm going to take a shower. Unless you want to first."

I breathe out. Loudly. I fake cough so she doesn't notice. "No, that's okay. I shower in the morning."

"Cool. That's easy." Summer grabs a bathrobe, towel, and shower caddy out of her closet and twirls toward the door.

The second the bedroom door shuts, the FaceTime ringtone blares through my iPad. I leap to my desk, grab it, and climb into the farthest corner of the bed, wrapping my comforter around it to try and muffle the noise.

"There's our little Mainer." Dad's face pops up on the screen.

"Hi, hon," Mom says. "How was your first official day?"

I lower the volume so I can barely hear them.

"Hi, guys," I whisper.

Dad squints and cups his hand around his ear. "I can barely hear you, Bea."

"Oh, sorry." I speak a tiny bit louder. "I don't want to disturb my roommate. She's uhhhhh . . . she's trying to study."

Mom and Dad nod approvingly.

"My first day was great. I really like it here." Kids are talking in the hallway, and I glance at the bedroom door, but it stays shut.

"Tell us all about it," Mom says.

"What's your favorite class?" Dad asks.

"We're studying ancient Greece in social studies. That's pretty cool. And we played softball in PE."

"Did you show them the Miller Spitter?" Dad winds his arm in a pitching motion.

"No, Dad." I force a smile. "You don't want me giving away all your secrets, do you?"

"The Miller Spitter's my favorite," Mom chimes in. "You always get the cutest look on your face when you throw that pitch."

"Awwww, thanks, babe," Dad says, and then he adds a kissy noise.

"Gross. Cut it out, you guys." I roll my eyes. I hate it when they get all mushy.

"How's the food?" Dad asks.

"It's really good. There are a million choices. They even have a humungo salad bar."

"Sounds great," Mom says. "Maybe we should move there."

I hear voices coming from the hallway again, but this time, one of them is Summer's.

I fake yawn. "Well, I'm pretty tired. I should go to bed."

"Already?" Mom asks. "You never go to bed this early."

Summer's laugh echoes through the hall.

"Yeah, but it's been a long day." I stretch my arms above my head. "I'm wiped out."

"Okay, Bea," Dad says. "We don't want to keep you up, but we'd love to hear more about your new school."

"I know, Dad. And I'd love to tell you. It's just that I'm really tired tonight." My eyes flash to the bedroom door.

"We're going to hold you to that," Mom says. "You can tell us more tomorrow night."

"I will. I promise."

The bedroom doorknob turns.

"Good night, Bea. I love you."

"Love you too."

The bedroom door opens.

"Good night!" I slam the iPad cover over the screen.

"Did you say something?" Summer asks. Her hair is dripping onto her bathrobe, which is hot pink plaid flannel.

"Me? No." I slide the tablet under the blankets.

"Oh, I thought I heard you talking in here." Summer shrugs.

"So, what time do you get up?" I change the subject.

"Breakfast is from seven to eight. Then we have to be in class by eight fifteen.

"Sounds good. So you don't mind if I get up a little earlier to shower?"

"Not at all." Summer crawls into bed and flicks her

reading light on. "This is your room too, so you don't have to ask me if you can do stuff. Make yourself at home."

"Thanks," I say. I pull out my book and pretend to read. Really I'm wondering how I'm going to find the time to talk to my parents tomorrow night. They'll freak out if I blow them off again. I need to find a way to talk to them for half an hour every night without anyone knowing. I squeeze my eyes shut. Think. Think. Think.

I come up with nothing. Except that I wish Summer took longer showers.

# Chapter ★10★

I WAKE UP TO DAYLIGHT WITH ADELE BLARING FROM my phone. I hit snooze and pull the covers over my head.

I peer out of the blankets just enough to see that Summer's still fast asleep. Maybe showering at night isn't such a bad idea.

The alarm blares again. As I pick up my phone to shut it off, I notice a text from Sophie.

Did u leave school? Nobody knows what happened 2 u. I'm worried. Call me ASAP.

I squeeze my eyes shut. This is not what I want to think about first thing in the morning. I block her number so I don't have to think about her ever again.

I push the covers off and stumble out of bed. I grab my bathrobe, towel, and shower caddy (which is so full of shampoo, conditioner, soap, and body wash that it must weigh at least ten pounds) and slowly open the bedroom door. I peek toward the bathroom but don't see anyone. The hallway's pretty quiet, so I scamper to the showers. I push open the bathroom door, hoping there's not a line. I'd hate to be late on my first official full day. Amazingly enough, I'm the only one in there. Just in case, though, I do a quick change out of my pj's and jump in the shower, not waiting for it to warm up. I jump back and adjust the temperature. I'm in there for five minutes when I hear people talking in the bathroom. Someone turns on the shower next to mine, and then someone else turns on the one next to that. I soap up as fast as I can, rinse, and then turn the shower off. I give myself a quick dry, throw my bathrobe on, and make my way out of the shower.

Just as I'm about to leave the bathroom, Cassandra walks in, wearing a knee-length fuzzy white bathrobe. I smile at her, but she doesn't say anything. In fact, she hardly looks at me at all. Maybe she's not a morning person. Or maybe she's not an anytime-of-day person.

When I open the door to our room, Summer is already awake and dressed in striped leggings and a T-shirt that says I <3 BEING AWESOME.

"How was your shower?"

"Not too bad. A little cold."

"They take forever to heat up."

I open my closet door and pull out my suitcase. There aren't too many choices, but luckily I packed one of my favorite dresses—one I made using old T-shirts. I've never shared a room before so I'm not sure if Summer would be okay with me getting dressed in front of her. Just in case, I decide to change in the closet. After slipping into the dress, I squeeze half a tube of de-frizzing gel into my hand—my hair hasn't yet adjusted to the East Coast dampness.

I step out of the closet as Summer spins around the room.

"Whooooooaaaaaa," Summer says when she stops spinning. "Cool dress."

"Oh, thanks." I feel my ears burn. "It's just something I made out of—"

"You *made* that?" Summer takes a step closer to me, still staring at the dress.

"Yeah, but it's no big deal."

"Are you kidding me? It is *such* a big deal." She touches the hem. "Can you make me one?"

"You really want one?" I ask.

"Totally." She's still staring at the dress. "Only make mine more crazy."

I laugh. "Okay! Do you have old T-shirts we can use?"

"Only boxes of them! I'll have my mom bring them tomorrow."

Nobody's ever commented on my designs before. Well, nobody's ever really seen them, except Ellie and my parents, and they never even noticed. I didn't wear any of my dresses to my old school because only designer labels were allowed in the building. I'm pretty sure that was written in the school handbook.

"Ready for breakfast?" Summer puts on shoes that are half sneakers, half boots. They're laced up the front with rainbow laces and totally clash with her striped leggings, but I think that's the point.

"Almost," I say. I slip on a peach-colored shrug sweater that falls just above my waist, then check the mirror one more time to put on some lip gloss. I contemplate mascara but then remember that the only other seventh-grader I've seen wearing makeup at Midcoast Academy is Cassandra, and I'm not sure I want to be anything like her.

Luckily, we don't see Cassandra at breakfast. Summer and I both get the blueberry pancakes, which she polishes off in about five minutes. For someone so small, she sure eats a lot. Connor and Shane come in just as we're leaving. Connor smiles at Summer and gives me a little wave. My stomach flutters, and I'm pretty sure it made some stupid gurgling sound. I hope Connor didn't hear it.

I have first period science with Summer—and Connor. Mr. Desmond gives me a textbook, and I take the only empty seat there is—behind Connor. Mr. Desmond draws a picture of a plant on the whiteboard. He's talking about the parts of the plant, which thankfully I already know from my old school. We did this unit last month, so my mind's free to wander. And it wanders to the seat in front of me.

Connor's light brown hair is just touching the collar of his Boston Celtics T-shirt. His knee is bouncing up and down, and every few minutes he taps his pencil on his notebook. He's not doing anything exciting, but for some reason, I can't stop staring at the back of his head.

I jump when the bell rings. There is no way that class is over. I look at the clock. Yep. I've been staring at the back of Connor's head for forty-five minutes. Luckily, Connor isn't in all my classes, or I'd completely fail out of Midcoast Academy.

I don't see Connor at lunch because he's in the astronomy club and they meet every Tuesday during lunch. I wonder what the astronomy club does.

After classes are over, Summer, Katie, and I head to the library to do our homework.

Cassandra walks with us, but when she sees Connor and Shane on the basketball court, she makes a beeline for them. Today she's wearing boots with two-inch heels. They're really pretty—black leather ankle boots with a fur-lined top—but I don't know how she's going to play basketball in them.

We're almost finished with our homework when Connor

walks into the library, a backpack on one shoulder and a basketball under one arm.

"Hey." He sits down next to Summer and takes a book out of his backpack. I look up and smile, but he's not looking at me.

"Hey," Summer says. She's quieter than normal. This must be her library voice. "Did you kick Shane's butt?"

"Yeah." Connor smiles. "I don't know why he always thinks he can beat me. He hasn't yet."

"How much homework do you have? We have to meet my parents in an hour."

"Not much. I can't wait for Clara's. I'm starving."

"Clara's has the most amazing lobster roll," Summer whispers to me.

"Yum," I say. I have no idea what a lobster roll is. I picture shellfish doing somersaults.

Summer nods her head and rubs her belly. "I can't wait."

"Me neither." I glance at Connor. His head is buried in his book.

"Let's meet at the usual place at five." Summer starts packing up her backpack.

"Sounds good," Connor says. He looks at me real fast and then looks back down at his book.

I'm so excited to have dinner with Summer and Connor that I hardly even worry about how I'm going to FaceTime my parents tonight—although it's always hanging over my head like the threat of rain on a cloudy day.

At five, Summer and I make our way to the main entrance lobby. Summer plops down on a brown leather couch next to the front desk, and I sit down next to her smoothing my skirt, which lands just above my knees. I want to look nice for Summer's parents. And Connor. But mostly Summer's parents.

Connor walks in a few minutes after us. He's talking with an older girl, and I realize, after my jaw hurts, that I'm clenching my teeth. Older Girl is laughing at something Connor's saying, and her brown curls are bouncing up and down. She's completely adorable, and based on her cargo pants and plain brown sweatshirt, she isn't even trying to be. Connor sits on the couch next to Summer, and Older Girl sits on Summer's lap.

"You weigh a ton." Summer squirms out from underneath her. "Get off of me."

Older Girl laughs and stands up. She looks at me with a great big smile on her face. "Hi. I'm Holly, Summer's sister."

I instantly relax. Older Girl is Summer's sister. Of course. *That's* why she's here talking to Connor.

"I'm Bea." I stand up.

"Nice to meet you, Bea. Welcome to Midcoast."

Summer and her sister look nothing alike, which is why I didn't immediately realize they were sisters. Holly has brown curly hair, while Summer's is straight and blond. Summer has blue eyes; Holly's are brown. They both have the same cute little nose, which I have to admit, I'm a little jealous of. I have Mom's wide nose, which works really well on *her* face.

Mrs. Kearney comes out of her office, briefcase in hand. "Clara's Café tonight?"

"Yes, Mrs. Kearney," Holly says.

"How are you adjusting to life at Midcoast?" Mrs. Kearney asks me as she locks her office door.

"It's great." I smile.

"I'm glad you like it. It must be quite different than home."

*Oh no. Of course Mrs. Kearney knows who my parents are. They registered me!*

Sweat breaks out on my forehead, and I try to think of something to say to change the subject, but my mind is blank. I hold my breath, waiting for her to say something else and blow my cover.

"Can we bring you back a lobster roll?" Holly asks.

I exhale.

Mrs. Kearney laughs. "No thanks, Holly, but you're sweet to ask. Say hi to your folks for me."

"We will," Holly says. "Have a good night."

Summer rolls her eyes and whispers to me, "Holly's the ninth grade class president. That's why she's so insanely friendly with everyone who works here."

I nod as if this makes perfect sense. All I know is that Holly just saved my life.

The front door opens, and Summer leaps off the couch toward the two people who walk in. They must be her parents. I stand and subtly floof my hair.

"Mommy!" Summer hugs her mom, who looks exactly like Holly in older form, and then she hugs her Dad, who looks exactly like Summer in man form. Holly hugs them next, and I just stand by the couch smiling like a dork. I fold my hands in front of me but realize that looks a little creepy, so I force my arms to just hang at my side.

Summer's mom gives Connor a hug, and Summer's dad shakes his hand.

"You must be Bea." Summer's mom comes toward me with her arms outstretched.

"Nice to meet you," I say after she releases me from a hug.

"We're so happy you'll be joining us," Summer's mom says. "I'm Veronica, and this is Eric." She motions to Summer's dad, who gives me a handshake instead of a hug.

"It's finally getting nice outside, so we thought we'd walk, if that's okay with you, Bea," Eric says.

"Sure," I say. I'm glad I wore my Converses—comfortable but fashionable and the spot-on choice with my T-shirt dress.

"Look at Bea's dress, Mom," Summer says. "She made it."

"You made that?" Veronica holds the door open for us, and we all pile out onto the walkway.

"Yes." I look down at my sneakers. She probably thinks it's ridiculous.

"Wow," Veronica says. "You're really talented."

I jerk my head up and smile uncontrollably. Nobody has ever called me talented before. Nobody ever. When you're the daughter of a supermodel-turned–television star and the best pitcher in the major leagues, regular, everyday talent doesn't look too interesting.

"That's why I needed the T-shirts." Summer grabs a shopping bag out of Veronica's hand. "Thanks for bringing them!"

The smile is still glued to my face as we walk into town. Holly's walking behind us with her parents. Summer, as usual, is skipping ahead. Which means I'm walking with Connor. I wipe my sweaty palms on my dress and give myself a pat on the back for making the dress out of cotton.

"You'll love Clara's," Connor says.

"It's good?" I ask, and give myself a mental face palm. *Of course it's good, Ruby. He just said you'd love it.*

"It's my favorite restaurant in town." Connor either doesn't notice my stupid question or he chooses to ignore it.

"It's really nice of Summer's parents to take us out."

"Oh yeah, they're awesome." Connor pauses. "When did it happen?"

I glance at him. "When did what happen?"

"Your parents." He's looking down at the sidewalk. "When did they—when did they pass away?"

Uh-oh. The neurons in my brain are firing blanks. I can't think of an answer. Did I tell Summer when they pretend "died"? I don't remember! And I have to be sure to keep my story straight if—

"I'm sorry." Connor hangs his head even lower than it was before. "That was rude of me to ask."

"Oh, no—not at all," I stammer. "It's just that I—I don't remember much about it. Them. I was really little."

Connor nods.

"How about you?" I don't really want to talk about dead parents, but since he asked about mine, I guess I should ask about his.

"I was six." He pushes his hair out of his eyes.

"Wow." I look over at him, but he's not looking at me. "How'd it happen?"

"Car accident."

"Wow."

"How about you?"

"What?"

"How did your parents die?"

Oh, right.

"Um, same." I can't think of anything else to say, so I say the first thing that pops into my mind. How could I be so stupid? I could have said something else. *Anything* else. Fire, plane crash, train wreck, deadly virus, killer bees. But no, I don't think of those other things fast enough, so not only does Connor think that we both have dead parents, but he also thinks they died the same way. This can't be good.

"Sucks, doesn't it?" This time he looks at me. *Right* at me.

"Totally," I say.

# Chapter

## ★ 11 ★

I LEARN TWO NEW THINGS TONIGHT. LOBSTER ROLLS are to die for. And Parents' Weekend is six weeks away.

"Is your nana coming up?" Summer asks. "If she isn't, you can hang with us."

"I'm not sure," I say. "I haven't talked to her about it. I didn't even know there was a Parents' Weekend."

"It's a huge deal at Midcoast. You'll see." Summer takes a bite of her second lobster roll.

"Summer, don't freak her out," Holly says.

"What? It is a big deal. There's the Spotlight Project, and of course the dance. That's the best part." As much as I dread finding a way to keep my parents away from Parents' Weekend, I'm kinda excited about the dance. I've never been to a school dance before.

After dinner we roll ourselves out of Clara's and make our way back to the dorms. We pass the chocolate shop and the ice cream shop, but I'm too stuffed to want to stop.

"Check it out, Mom." Holly points to a newsstand next door to the ice cream shop. "*National Geographic*'s ocean issue is out." She runs over to the magazine and immediately flips through it.

Summer rolls her eyes. "Have you ever seen anyone get so excited about whales?"

I laugh, until I notice that Summer, Connor, and I are right in front of the tabloid section. And smack in front of my nose is *Celebrity Scuttlebutt* magazine. And who's on the cover of *Celebrity Scuttlebutt* this month? Zack Miller, Celestine Cruz, and their daughter—whose face is hidden in this particular picture—leaving Sarriette's.

I can taste the lobster roll coming back up, but there's no way I can puke now. *Breathe, Ruby.* I close my eyes and take a deep breath in. I have to get everyone out of here. Now. Before someone decides to flip through *Celebrity Scuttlebutt.* What if there's a photo of me inside? I do a quick check of everyone's location. Holly and her mom are still looking at *National Geographic.* Eric is reading something in *Newsweek.* Summer and Connor are still right next to me, and I'm still right in front of *Celebrity Scuttlebutt.*

Without thinking, I point to the magazine rack that's as far away as possible from the tabloids. "Wow! Look at that!"

"What?" Summer asks, following the direction of my finger.

I walk toward the rack, with my finger pointing.

"*Popular Mechanics*?" Connor asks.

"Uhhhh." Yep, I'm in the car section. "Yeah. Cool, right?"

"I didn't know you liked engines." Connor was beaming.

"Well, I don't. I mean, I do, but . . . it's just that I love the picture on the cover." Great. Another lie.

"What is it?" Summer cocks her head to one side, as if looking at the cover from a different angle will help her figure it out.

I purse my lips. I have no idea what it is. It's just a bunch of metal parts clumped together in the shape of a snail.

"It's a turbocharger," Connor says, as if everyone knows that.

"Yeah, it's a turbocharger." I nod. "A nice one."

Connor looks at me and smiles. "I'm impressed that you know what that is."

I wave my hand in front of my face, desperate to end this conversation and leave the newsstand. But Connor's distracted by another magazine, and we follow him to the next rack.

"It's the new issue of *Astronomy*." He picks it up and stares at the cover, which shows a photo of a giant telescope.

"How cool would this be for the observation deck?" Connor asks Summer.

"That'd be awesome." Her eyes are as big as the telescope.

"I'm putting together plans to build an observation deck off the science room," Connor explains. "Summer's dad is helping me."

"That's really cool," I say. Before I can say anything else, Summer's mom waves us over.

"You guys ready?" she asks.

"Yep!" I'm the first one back on the sidewalk.

We're about a block past the newsstand when the back of my neck sprouts sprinklers. What happens if someone from Midcoast goes to that newsstand and looks inside *Celebrity Scuttlebutt*? What happens if I'm in there? I've got to get rid of those magazines. And I've got to get rid of them now—before it's too late.

"Uh-oh." I stop walking. Everyone else stops too. "I think I dropped some money out of my pocket. Must have been while we were at the newsstand."

"That's okay, Bea," Veronica says. "We can go back and look. It's only a block—"

"No, I'll go." I turn around and break into a light jog. "I'll be right back."

"We'll come with you." Summer starts running to catch me.

"No, really, I'll be right back." And I run faster than I've ever run before.

Every few seconds I glance behind me to be sure nobody's following. They're not. Not yet anyway.

There's a huge stack of *Celebrity Scuttlebutt* magazines, and I quickly realize I can't hide them all. I run up to the cashier, breathless.

"How many of those do you have?" I point to the stack.

"Whatever's there," he says.

I peek my head down the block to be sure nobody's coming. "I'll take all of them."

"All of them? I don't even know how many are there. It will take me a minute to count them."

"I don't have a minute. How many do you think there are?"

The cashier walks over to the stack and starts counting. "Probably about seventy-five. Maybe one hundred."

"And how much are they?" I pull my wallet out of my purse.

"Three dollars each."

I try to do the math in my head. I'm figuring one hundred magazines because I want to make sure I get all of them, and anyway, one hundred is way easier to multiply by three than seventy-five.

I pull out my credit card and shove it into the cashier's hand "Just put three hundred dollars on there."

Another peek down the street, and I see that Summer and Connor are walking this way.

# Chapter
## ✦ 12 ✦

THE CASHIER LOOKS AT ME THROUGH SQUINTY EYES and hands me my receipt. "Can you carry all of those?"

"I don't need to," I say. "Can you just take them all, and throw them away?"

"You want me to throw them away?"

"Yes." I nod so hard my head hurts. Connor and Summer are getting closer.

He shrugs. "Okay, you bought 'em."

"Thank you." I turn to go, and I bump into Connor so hard that I almost knock him down.

"Did you find your money?" he asks.

"Yep." I tap my purse. "All fine now."

I smile at Summer and Connor and hope there's not sweat dripping off my nose.

We catch up with Summer's parents, and they walk us back to the dorms. By the time we get there, my heart rate is almost back to normal. Summer's folks give us all hugs, and her mom reminds Holly and Summer to text or call every night.

"We always do," Holly says.

"So do you talk to your parents every night?" I ask Summer when we're back in our room.

"Yeah, either that or text. It was the only way Mom would let us board here. We live so close that Holly was a day student for a while. I wasn't old enough to come here yet, so I went to our town's public school. Holly was always saying she missed out on the fun, so when it was time for me to start middle school, we begged my parents to let us board. Dad was cool with it but Mom wouldn't budge. Finally, when we promised we'd text or call every single day and have dinner once a week and even come home once in a while on weekends, she agreed."

I wonder if my parents would go for texting instead of FaceTime. It would make my life a lot easier. Speaking of my parents, I look at my phone. I have an hour until eight o'clock. I can't wait until my boxes from home arrive. At least then I'll have headphones.

"Well, I'm going to shower." Summer kicks off her shoes and throws them in her closet.

"Already?" I jump in front of her. I need her to wait an hour.

She gives me a funny look. "Why not?"

"I thought, uhhhh, well, I thought we'd go through some of the T-shirts your mom brought. You know, to pick out the ones you want for your ultra-crazy dress."

Summer breaks out into a huge smile. "Great idea."

We sit on the floor, and she flings T-shirts into two piles. Only the really colorful ones make it into the pile for the dress.

"You should totally apply for the Parents' Weekend Spotlight Project. You could submit your designs." Summer flings a neon-green-striped shirt into the dress pile.

"What's a Spotlight Project?" I ask.

"Every Parents' Weekend, we display projects we've been working on. It doesn't have to be stuff we do in school. It could be things we do on our own time. Each year, one person gets picked for the Spotlight Project, which parents and teachers make a really big deal of. Plus, you get a hundred-dollar prize. Holly got chosen for the Spotlight Project last year. She built a biodome. It was filled with snails and frogs and pond scum."

"Pond scum?" I wrinkle my nose.

"Holly loves pond scum."

I furrow my eyebrows.

"She wants to be a marine biologist. That's why she freaks out about whales."

"Ahhhh," I say.

"Anyway, you should totally apply for this year's Spotlight Project!"

"Oh, I don't know. My dresses really aren't that great."

"The one you're wearing is amazing." Summer jumps up. "Do you have other ones you've made?"

"I have a bunch, but this is the only one I packed in my suitcase. The rest of my stuff should be here tomorrow, I hope."

"Cool." Summer focuses on the T-shirt pile again. "I can't wait till your stuff gets here."

I wonder if she'll like my other dresses as much as she likes the one I'm wearing. What if she hates them? Then she'll realize I'm a one-hit wonder, and this one was just a fluke. I bite the inside of my cheek.

"Hopefully your nana can come to Parents' Weekend, especially if you're the Spotlight Project," Summer says.

"Oh yeah. I'll tell her about it."

"You won't even have to. The school starts sending e-mails and invitations home way in advance. Mom mentioned that she got one today."

"They send stuff to our parents?" My stomach flip-flops and I add, "Or guardian?"

"Yep. I'm telling you, it's a really big deal. I'll bet your nana comes. Even Connor's uncle comes."

"His uncle?" The sound of Connor's name takes my attention away from the fact that my pretend-dead parents may or may not have already received an invitation to Parents' Weekend.

"Yeah, he's the one who took Connor after his parents died. He lives in Boston. Connor hated it there. His uncle works all the time so he never saw him. It was really hard on him, being so little and alone." Summer tilts her head. "Well, you know."

She looks like she's waiting for me to say something. I don't know what to say because I really *don't* know, so I just nod and look sad. I'm not even faking it, either. Thinking of poor little Connor all alone really does make me sad.

"So he's not close with his uncle?"

"No." Summer shakes her head. "They hardly see each other. Connor's uncle sends him to camp during summer break, and hardly ever visits him at school."

I want to ask Summer more about Connor, but she changes the subject before I get the chance.

"Enough shirts to make the dress?" Summer admires the T-shirt pile.

"Yep, that's plenty."

"Where do you want them?" Summer piles the T-shirts in her arms. I hold open a paper bag, and she dumps them all in.

"You can put them next to my desk, and I'll start on the dress this week."

"Really? You sure you don't mind?" Summer's bouncing on her toes.

"Not at all. It'll be fun!"

"Thanks! You're a great friend, Bea."

Hearing her call me a great friend makes me smile so hard my mouth hurts. But there's a tiny pull in my stomach, reminding me that a great friend wouldn't lie about her parents being dead.

"I'm going to hop in the shower." Summer grabs her shower gear. My heart races, until I look at the clock on my desk: 7:58. Perfect timing.

"Okay." I sit down and uncover my iPad. "I'm just going to check my e-mail."

Summer closes the bedroom door, and my parents ring in about five seconds later. My shoulders relax. Maybe this won't be so hard after all.

Mom and Dad appear in their little boxes on my screen, and I instantly launch into my day. Based on last night's shower, I have about fifteen minutes, and I want to be sure I tell them everything so they won't get suspicious. I fill them in on Greek democracy, the anatomy of a plant, and the fact that I will never, ever understand how to read music. I tell them about Clara's Café and lobster rolls and Summer's family. We talk about the weather and Mom's taping and Dad's practice. The only thing I don't bring up is Parents' Weekend.

"I'm so glad things are going well, hon," Mom says.

Just as I'm about to tell them that I have to get ready for

bed, the door to our room swings open. Before I can think to cover the iPad, I turn around to find Cassandra standing in our doorway—staring right at me. A million scenarios shoot through my mind in three seconds flat. I could turn the iPad off, but my parents would freak out. I could turn the screen around, but that would look suspicious. Instead I press the mute button and place the iPad on my lap, silently praying that she can't see the screen from where she's standing. My parents will probably wonder why they're staring at the ceiling, and why I'm not answering them, but right now this is my best possible option.

Cassandra's eyes move past me. She's trying to look at the screen, which I'm covering with my arms.

"Whatcha doing?" Cassandra asks. She's still standing in the doorway.

"Homework."

"Where's Summer?" Cassandra looks around the room.

"She's in the shower."

Cassandra squints. "Do you remember what the Spanish homework was?"

"We didn't have any."

"You sure?" Her eyes shoot to my lap, so I lean over the screen even more.

"Positive."

"Do you know if Summer talked to Connor about me?"

The back of my neck feels sticky with sweat. I need to

get back to my parents. They've got to be wondering what the heck is going on. Besides, Summer will be out of the shower any minute now, and I have to say good night to my parents before that.

"I don't know. Want to swing by the bathroom and ask her?"

"I'll just talk to her tomorrow." Cassandra tries to look at my iPad screen again and smirks. "Have fun with your homework." She turns on her heels and shuts the door behind her.

I exhale and unmute my parents. "Sorry." I give them a totally fake smile.

"What was that about?" Mom asks.

"Oh, just some girl wanting to know about homework. She's kind of annoying, so . . ."

"We were wondering what was going on over there. It didn't seem like you could hear us," Dad says.

"I couldn't," I say. "That girl—she's really loud."

"As long as everything's okay," Mom says, looking worried.

"Oh yeah, it's great. There is one thing, though." I bite the inside of my cheek.

"Sure, Bea," Dad says.

"It's not always easy to get on FaceTime," I say. "I'd hate to disturb my roommate, and sometimes the Internet's slow here at night. . . ."

I know my parents are thousands of miles away, but I swear it feels like they can *smell* my lies.

"Any chance we can text at night—instead of FaceTime?"

Now Mom and Dad are having a psychic conversation. It always amazes me that they can do this through the computer just as well as they can do it in person.

"I think it's hard enough that we're not going to see you in person every month, Bea," Dad finally says. "We'd hate to give up seeing you through FaceTime."

"And that was part of our deal," Mom reminds me. "You could go to boarding school as long as you keep up with your grades—and we talk every night."

"I know," I say. "And it's not that I don't want to. It's just that—my roommate texts her parents every night. And so do most kids here."

The psychic conversation resumes. I just sit back and wait for it to end. It's twelve minutes after eight so I hope it ends quickly.

"Let's stick with FaceTime for now, hon," Mom says.

"Yeah, Bea, we'd miss your face too much if we didn't." Dad smiles. It's hard to be mad at Dad when he smiles. I can see why all those crazy women always throw flowers onto the field whenever he's up at bat.

I hear Summer's voice in the hallway again, and I'm grateful that she stops to chat with everyone hanging out in the hall. I have about one minute to sign off, but I try not to make it too obvious that I want this call to end.

"Okay." I nod. "FaceTime it is. I'd better wrap it up here. It's lights out at nine and I'm nowhere near ready for bed. I love you guys."

"We love you too," Mom says. Dad makes kissy noises. I can still hear Summer in the hallway.

I turn the iPad off and put my head in my hands. That thing with Cassandra was too close. I'm pretty sure she didn't see anything, but what if she did? Or what if she does next time? Everyone's heard by now that my parents are supposedly dead.

All of a sudden I'm exhausted. I've got to find a way to convince my parents to let me text instead of FaceTime. Thank goodness they didn't say anything about Parents' Weekend. Maybe they didn't get the e-mail because I just registered. Maybe I'm not even on the e-mail distribution list yet.

When Summer comes back, I tell her that Cassandra stopped by.

"What did she want?"

"She asked if there was Spanish homework. And then she asked if you spoke to Connor about her."

Summer rolls her eyes but doesn't say anything. I wonder if she did ask Connor about Cassandra, but if I ask her, she'll wonder why I'm wondering.

"So yeah, she said she'd talk to you tomorrow."

"Can't wait," Summer mumbles.

I purse my lips together to stop myself from asking Summer a zillion questions about Connor and Cassandra. I just got to Midcoast—I shouldn't be *this* curious about anybody yet. But then, Connor isn't just anybody. He's probably the nicest boy I've ever met.

*Yank.*

There's that tug on my stomach again, reminding me that the nicest boy I've ever met doesn't deserve to be lied to.

# Chapter
## ★ 13 ★

CASSANDRA AND KATIE ARE ALREADY AT BREAKFAST by the time Summer and I come in. Cassandra calls us over even before we get in the cafeteria line. Summer waves to her as if she didn't hear a word she said, then she picks up a tray and hands it to me.

"Sheesh. She can wait until we eat at least," Summer says under her breath.

We get our scrambled eggs and potatoes and sit down with Cassandra and Katie.

"Did you talk to Connor at dinner last night?" Cassandra's blotting her lip gloss on a napkin.

"No, my parents were there the whole time."

"So?" Cassandra crosses her arms across her chest.

"My parents don't want to hear that stuff." Summer eats a forkful of potatoes.

"Can you talk to him today?"

"I dunno. Maybe," Summer says. "If there's a good time."

"I want him to ask me to the Spring Fling." Cassandra leans back in her chair.

"There's still almost a month and a half till the Spring Fling," Summer says. "That's plenty of time."

"What if he asks somebody else," Cassandra says.

Summer laughs. "Who's he going to ask?"

"You never know." Cassandra glances my way for a split second, and my cheeks feel super hot.

"I promise you," Summer says. "Connor isn't even thinking about the Spring Fling."

"How do you know?" Cassandra asks.

"I know him. Right now he's probably thinking about the Sox."

"He's thinking about his socks?" Cassandra twists her hair around her finger.

"Do you actually know anything about Connor?" Summer tears the crust off her toast.

"I know he's hot," Cassandra says. Katie giggles.

"He's a huge Red Sox fan and baseball season is starting," Summer says. "That's the most important thing on his mind right now."

"Baseball is *so* boring," Cassandra says.

"I love baseball," I say. The words slip out before I can stop them. My dad's been captain of the Dodgers for over a decade. I was practically born in their dugout.

"Baseball's pretty fun," Summer says, and then turns to Cassandra. "Maybe you should get to know him a little better before deciding you want to go to the Spring Fling with him."

"I know all I need to know." Cassandra stands up, and Katie follows. "Just talk to him, okay?"

Summer sighs.

Cassandra smiles, her perfect teeth practically blinding me. "Thanks, babe. TTYL," she says, and glides out of the cafeteria.

Just as we're about to clear off our trays, Connor walks in. He sits down next to Summer.

"Hey," he says. He looks at me first, for like a second, and then at Summer.

"Okay, so I have to ask you something." Summer turns toward him.

"What?" Connor takes a sip of orange juice.

"Cassandra wants you to ask her to the Spring Fling. Will you?"

Connor's face looks like he just swallowed a lemon. Either his orange juice has gone bad, or he doesn't want to ask Cassandra out. I'm hoping and praying the orange juice is fine.

"Seriously?" he says.

Summer raises her eyebrows.

"I don't like her," he says.

I bite my lip to stop the gigantic smile creeping across my face.

"Yeah, I figured, but I told her I'd ask so I'm asking."

"She wears way too much makeup." Connor takes a bite of an egg sandwich. My hand instinctively goes to my lips. I'm relieved when I realize I forgot to put on lip gloss this morning. I decide right then and there that I will never, ever use lip gloss again. At least not until I'm in seventh grade.

"Plus," Connor says, "we have nothing in common."

"I tried to tell her that," Summer says. "But she thinks you're hot." She rolls her eyes and laughs. "Anyway, Holly says sixth graders can't be hot. She says they can be cute, but not hot."

"I must be very, very cute, then." Connor is cracking up. I can't help but giggle.

"So what should I tell her?" Summer asks.

"I don't know," Connor says. "Tell her I don't dance."

"I don't know why she's making such a big deal of this. It's not that—"

"Summer!" Holly's running over to our table. "I need my notebook."

"What notebook?" Summer asks.

"The blue one you borrowed yesterday? You forgot to give it back to me."

"Oh, right!" Summer exclaims. "I left it in my room."

"Well, let's go get it. Class starts in ten minutes."

"See you guys in class." Summer stands up and pushes in her chair. Holly smiles and waves at us, but I can tell she's in a hurry.

Connor and I are sitting alone at the table. Connor and I. Alone.

My cheeks feel like they're so pink I want to pour my glass of water over my head, but since that isn't really an option, I take a sip. "So the Spring Fling's a dance?"

"Oh, yeah," Connor says. "Sorry, I forgot you don't know what we were talking about. It's the big dance party the night before Parents' Weekend."

"That sounds fun."

"It should be."

We both nod.

Connor puts jam on his toast. I try to look busy drinking my water.

"The rest of Parents' Weekend is pretty cool, but—well, you know. It can be hard to see everyone having fun with their parents," Connor says between bites of toast.

"Yeah," I say. "I'm sure." *Yank.*

"Is your grandma going to come?"

I shrug. "I'm not sure. How about your uncle?"

"He might show up. But if he doesn't, Summer's parents are awesome. They'll treat us like family."

"They seem really nice." I'm tearing my napkin to shreds.

"So you really don't remember them, huh?" Connor asks. And I realize he's not talking about Summer's parents. He's talking about mine.

I can't answer this question. Of course I remember my parents. Especially since I just saw them, but I can't tell Connor that. And I can't lie either. So I just shrug.

"I'm not sure if I do," Connor says.

"What do you mean?" I put the pieces of my napkin on my tray.

"Well, I think I remember them. But I'm not sure if it's them I remember, or if it's pictures of them, or if I'm just making up memories."

"Yeah," I say. I kinda know what he means because I feel that way about my grandma, who died when I was little. I've heard so many stories about her from Mom that I don't know what I remember about her, or what I know from the stories.

"Is your birthday in July?" Connor asks.

"What?" I'm thankful for the change of subject even if it does seem a little abrupt.

Connor looks at my neck, and I realize I'm fingering my necklace—the one with the ruby that my parents gave me for my birthday.

"Oh, no." I fold my hands in my lap. "My parents got me this—for my birthday. It's in March."

"It's nice," Connor says. "I only asked because my mom's birthday was in July. Her birthstone was a ruby and she always wore a ring with a ruby in it."

"Oh wow. It's amazing that you remember that."

"Yeah, it's weird the things you remember. You know?"

I nod.

"So why a ruby?"

My heart is beating so loudly I'm positive he can hear it. I'm afraid to say anything about my parents, because one slip will ruin it all. I take a deep breath, and speak slowly.

"My real name is Ruby, but my nickname is Bea."

"Oh, that's cool." Connor pushes the hair out of his eyes. I actually manage to look at him long enough to notice that his eyes are gray. But not a dull gray. More like a silver gray. Like the color of the chain on my necklace.

"It's nice that you have that to remember them by." He points at my necklace.

"Do you have anything—I mean—to remember your parents by?" I stammer.

Connor shakes his head. "Not really. My parents both came from small families. After they died, I moved in with my uncle, my dad's younger brother, who was just out of college. Honestly, he wasn't really ready to take care of me. When he cleaned out our old house, he only kept my stuff.

And pictures. So, at least I have pictures." His eyes look at me as he talks, but I can tell that he's seeing something completely different in his mind.

"It's good you have pictures," I say, and take another sip of water.

"Yeah, I'll show them to you one of these days. Do you have pictures of your folks?"

I almost choke on my water. "Oh, uhhh, a few. At home. At my nana's place." There is no way that I could ever show Connor—or anyone—pictures of my parents.

"I really want something else to remember them by. Something bigger. That's why I'm building the observation deck. I'm going to use the money they left me when they died, and then name it after them."

Before I can tell him how amazing that is, Connor looks at his watch and picks up his tray. "Whoa. I can't believe how late it is. We should get to class."

I'm finally able to relax after that conversation. I look around the cafeteria and notice that everyone else has already left. I pick my tray up and follow Connor over to the compost area.

"Hey, thanks for listening." Connor adds his tray to the stack of trays already there. "It's nice to be able to talk to somebody who understands, you know?"

I can't say anything, so as usual, I just smile and nod. Connor must think I'm a total dork who doesn't know how to speak. On the bright side, I guess being a total dork is better than being a total liar.

Connor and I don't speak much after breakfast, and I almost forget about the fact that I'm a lying dork by the time Summer and I get back to our dorm room after classes end. I open our door to find a stack of boxes next to my bed.

"Looks like your stuff came." Summer eyeballs the boxes.

A big smile spreads across my face. As much as I love it here at Midcoast, I do miss my stuff. I wonder what Ellie packed for me, and I grab a pair of scissors from my desk drawer to unpack the boxes. I'm just about to start on the biggest box when it hits me.

*I wonder what Ellie packed for me.*

What if she packed a bunch of photos from home? What if I open this box, right now, right in front of Summer, and there's a huge picture of my parents and me? I put the scissors down on my desk and pull a book out of my backpack instead.

"Aren't you going to open them?" Summer looks more excited to see my stuff than I am.

"Oh, yeah, it's just that I want to get this English assignment done first. All of a sudden I had a great idea about what to write and I don't want to forget."

Summer shrugs and looks a bit disappointed. "Okay."

Just as I sit down at my desk, there's a knock at the door.

"Come in," Summer says.

The door opens, and Ms. Goldberg peeks her head in. "Oh good, you got your stuff. I just wanted to make sure they brought it up."

"Yes, thank you," I say.

"Do you need any help unpacking? There are quite a few boxes here."

"Oh, no thanks. I'll probably do it later. It shouldn't take me long."

"Okay, but feel free to come get me if you need help."

"Don't worry, I'll help her." Summer shoots Ms. Goldberg a great big smile.

"I'm sure you will." Ms. Goldberg laughs. "I'm surprised you haven't dug into those boxes already."

"Bea wants to get her homework done first. So I will too." Summer reaches into her desk drawer and pulls out a pencil with a pink ball of fuzz on top.

"Nice! Looks like Bea will be a good influence on you," Ms. Goldberg says. "How's the math coming?"

Summer groans. "It isn't. It makes no sense."

"Do you need any help?"

"I don't know. I haven't opened the book yet."

Ms. Goldberg raises her eyebrows. Summer reaches into her backpack and pulls out a math book. She flashes Ms. Goldberg a smile.

"I'll leave you to your work, then. Let me know if you need any help." She gently closes the door behind her.

A second later there's another knock. This time the door swings open before we can even say anything.

Cassandra.

"Jeez, you can't just barge in here. What if one of us was changing or something?" Summer asks.

Cassandra just rolls her eyes and sits on Summer's bed. "Did you talk to Connor?"

Summer puts her pencil on the desk.

"Yes."

"Well, what'd he say?"

"He said he doesn't dance."

Cassandra folds her arms across her chest. "What?"

"He doesn't want to go to the dance with anybody. It's not personal. He just doesn't think it's the kind of thing you take a girl to."

Cassandra flips her hair and snorts. "Of course it's the kind of thing you take a girl to. It's a *dance*."

Summer shrugs. "That's what he said."

"Is that all he said?"

"Pretty much."

"Pretty much, or definitely?"

Summer picks up her pencil and taps the pink fuzz on her cheek. "Well, he did say that he didn't think you guys had a lot in common."

"He said that?"

"Pretty much."

"Pretty much, or definitely? What did he say, exactly?"

"I don't remember exactly." Summer throws her hands in the air. "I didn't video the entire conversation."

Cassandra stands up. "If Connor doesn't think we have anything in common, then I'll just have to prove him wrong."

"But he isn't wrong," Summer says.

"You leave that up to me," Cassandra huffs, and she's gone as quickly as she came in.

Summer and I look at each other and crack up.

"She's crazy." Summer shakes her head. "Connor will never like her."

I smile.

"You know what I think?" Summer is tapping her pencil against her desk now.

"What?"

"I think he likes you."

I turn around so fast that my arm knocks my books off of my desk, and they crash to the floor. I bend down to pick them up, which gives me the perfect excuse to hide my face so Summer can't see how red it is.

"Wh-what? No. Why do you think that?" I stammer as I put my books back on my desk. She smiles. "I can just tell."

"Did he—did he say something?" I keep my voice cool and steady.

"No, but he talks to you a lot."

"Yeah, but maybe he's just friendly." My stomach is flipping and flopping.

"He's not." Summer laughs.

"Well I—I don't think—"

"You guys do have a lot in common. You know, with your parents and all."

"That's not really enough of a reason to *like* someone, though. I mean, you know, there has to be more than that," I say.

"You both like baseball," Summer points out.

That part is true. But I don't think Connor even knows that I like baseball.

"Anyway, it's just a hunch. I could be wrong." Summer goes back to doing her homework, and I go back to pretending to do mine. There's no way I can concentrate on symbolism and metaphors now I know Connor might actually like me!

I replay my conversation with Summer over in my mind.

*I think he likes you. . . . You guys do have a lot in common.*

My stomach sinks into my socks when I remember that I'm not who Connor thinks I am. And, now that I'm thinking about it, *I'm* not even sure who I am. Am I Ruby, daughter of celebrities, or am I Bea, daughter of nobody?

# Chapter
## ★ 14 ★

I SCOOT OUT OF DINNER A LITTLE EARLY SO I CAN OPEN up my boxes without Summer there. I tell her I'm heading up to the room, and she volunteers to come with me. I whisper that I have to go to the bathroom, and trust me, she doesn't want to be anywhere in the vicinity, if she knows what I mean. She laughs and gives me a thumbs-up.

I tackle the boxes as soon as I get in the door, and it's a good thing, too. Right on top of the biggest box is a framed photo of me with my parents. I slip it under my mattress. In this box Ellie packed my clothes and shoes, a few books, Luke and Leia (my two favorite teddy bears), and my headphones.

"Yes!" I say out loud. At least if Summer does hear my conversations, she won't hear my parents on the other end.

I could just pretend I'm talking to Ellie or a friend back home.

I gasp when I open the next box. I didn't expect that Ellie would send me my fabric collection, but I'm thrilled that she did. I pull out a roll of hot pink chiffon silk that I got in India when Mom did a fashion show in New Delhi. Then I find a sheet of white Italian linen from Rome that I picked up when Dad filmed a cologne commercial there. On top of the rolls of fabric are my collection of accessories. There's the shabby-chic spool of ribbon from Paris, the antique brass buttons from a New York flea market, and a bag of sequins from a dress that Mom threw out years ago.

At the very bottom of the box is a design I started last year but never finished. I hold it close, touching the lace overlay against my cheek for a few seconds, then gently put it back where it came from—placing everything else carefully on top—and push the box under my bed.

I unpack my clothes and put them in my closet. I'm not sure how all my clothes will fit in here. At home my closet is the size of this entire room, which seems pretty crazy now. I pull out the silver dress I wore on my birthday, just as Summer opens the door.

"Whoa," she says. "That's an awesome dress."

"Thank you." I put it on a hanger. "It's one of the ones I made."

"No. Way." Summer's staring at it, her eyes wide. "You

made that?" She runs her hand over the soft, shimmering fabric.

"It was pretty easy, really. These sequins here were the only hard part." I point to the sequins on the straps.

"Bea, you *have t*o apply for the Spotlight Project. You have to."

"I don't think they're good enough to be *spotlighted*–"

"I just had the best idea!" Summer's bouncing up and down. "A fashion show! Instead of just submitting your designs, you should do a fashion show!"

"What do you mean? Like with models?"

"Totally! I'll be a model, and I'm sure Holly and her friends will do it too. I bet Katie and Cassandra would love to. Especially Cassandra. Just make sure she gets a fancy dress."

Now I'm bouncing up and down too. I imagine everyone looking at my clothes, thinking I actually have a talent. Maybe people would really like them?

"You really think so?" I ask Summer.

"Totally!" We hold hands and bounce up and down together.

"Okay, but I'm not even sure how to apply–"

"Don't worry. I'll help you," Summer promises. "It will be pure awesomeness."

We squeal and jump for several minutes, until Ms. Goldberg peeks her head in and asks us to keep the noise down. Summer helps me put away the rest of my stuff, and

I show her the other dresses I've made, which she completely goes crazy for. She's already decided who will wear what dress for the fashion show.

"I'll be the coordinator, so you don't have to worry about anything but designing dresses," she declares.

"But don't I first have to get accepted as the Spotlight Project?"

"Yeah, but you'll definitely win. No one else is doing anything as cool as this. Let's get working on the application now! The deadline is midnight tonight." Summer opens her computer. We log on to the student portal of Midcoast's website and click the Spotlight Project application button. There are a bunch of questions that are pretty easy, like "What is your project?" and "How will your project be displayed?" that I answer out loud while Summer types what I say. I'm a little stuck on "Why are you excited about this project?"

"That's a hard one to answer." I pace while Summer sits at the computer, fingers on keyboard, ready to type.

"Why? Just talk out loud about why you want to do this."

"Well," I begin. "I've always loved to draw dresses because clothes are like the wrapping paper on a present. They don't change what's inside, but they brighten up the outside." I don't tell her that I've been to more fashion shows than I can count, and, while the designs are always beautiful, they don't always make the person who wears them more beautiful.

"That's good!" Summer types what I say.

"Then, El—my nana—taught me how to sew, and that was nice because it was something we could do together, just the two of us."

"Keep going." Summer's fingers are flying across the keyboard.

"So, designing and making the dresses combined two things that I love: making people brighter and spending time with—with my nana." I almost say Ellie again.

"That's perfect!" Summer hits the submit button, and my application is complete.

I'm so excited about the possibility of winning the Spotlight Project spot that I don't even think about the fact that it will take place during Parents' Weekend. That is, until I talk with my parents.

"Hey, Bea," Dad says. I plug my headphones in, even though Summer is safely in the shower.

"Hi, Dad. Hi, Mom."

"Hi, baby. How was your day?"

"Great! My stuff came."

"Oh good," Mom says. "We got something today too."

"What's that?"

"An e-mail about Parents' Weekend."

I blink.

"Did you hear me, hon?" Mom says. "It sounds like our connection's cutting out."

"Yeah, I heard you. That's great. I've heard about Parents' Weekend. I think it's sometime in May."

"It is, but unfortunately the show doesn't go on hiatus until June, and your father will be in the middle of the season."

I suck my cheeks in so I don't smile. "Oh no. That's such a shame." I bite my lower lip, hoping that will make me look sad.

"We're so disappointed." Dad frowns.

"Me too," I say. "But don't worry about it. It's probably not that big a deal."

"I don't know." Mom shakes her head. "The e-mail made it seem like it was a big deal. Maybe we could find a way to change our schedules—"

I interrupt her before she can finish that sentence. "All e-mails make everything seem like a big deal, Mom. They probably hire somebody just to send out e-mails like that. I wouldn't worry about it."

"We don't want you to feel left out," Dad tells me. "What if you're the only kid there without parents in town?"

"I know for sure that I won't be." I smile so they know it's no big deal. "Really, don't worry about it. Summer already invited some of us to hang out with her parents, since they live close."

"So there are other parents who aren't coming?" Mom asks.

"Yeah, a bunch," I say. I don't know how many make up a

bunch, but I decide that me and Connor are, for the sake of this discussion, a bunch.

"Okay." Mom presses her lips together. "If you're sure."

"I'm sure." I nod.

"We really miss you, Bea," Dad says.

"I miss you guys too, but there's only two months left of school, and then I'll be home all summer. You'll be sick of me by July."

Mom and Dad laugh, and I can tell this crisis has been averted. We go on to talk about regular everyday stuff like my English paper and campus food. I don't mention the Spotlight Project application. Even though they've never shown any interest in my dresses, I don't want to give them *any* reason to show up.

I get off FaceTime just as Summer finishes her shower. Perfect timing. In fact, today's been a pretty perfect day. My boxes came, I might get to do a fashion show as the Spotlight Project, and my parents aren't coming for Parents' Weekend.

And the best part? Summer thinks Connor might like me.

Right now I'm way too pumped up to even worry about anyone finding out about my parents. I mean, I know it's wrong to lie, but it's not like I'm lying for no reason. I'm lying because it's the only way to know for sure that my friends like me for who I am. That's a big deal for someone in my situation. I decide that's the way I have to look at it from now on. I can't feel bad about it anymore. This is something I have to do. It's self-preservation. I practically have no choice.

As I wait to fall asleep, all I can think about are dress designs and boys with dimples.

# Chapter

## ⋆ 15 ⋆

I WAKE UP TO THE SOUND OF RAIN. IT'S SO DARK OUT-side that Summer and I have a hard time getting out of bed. We're even late for breakfast, so we each grab a bagel and bring it into our first period class, science. Luckily Mr. Desmond isn't here yet, so we have time to eat. I take my seat behind Connor, who gives me a cute little smile as I scoot past him. I unwrap my bagel and take a bite but almost spit it out when Cassandra walks in.

Cassandra is decked out like I've never seen her before. And not in her usual designer clothes and heels. She's covered—head to toe—in Boston Red Sox gear. Her red sweatpants have the words "RED SOX" embroidered down the leg. She has a blue T-shirt on with a big red *B* in the center of it. Her blue baseball cap matches her shirt. And she's wearing sneakers. Of course, these aren't regular sneakers—they're dressy sneakers with a cute little wedge heel—but *still*.

Summer's eyes don't leave Cassandra from the minute she walks in until the minute she sits down. Unfortunately, neither do Connor's.

"What are you wearing?" I hear Summer whisper to Cassandra.

"It's opening day today." Cassandra's bright red lip gloss matches the *B* on her shirt perfectly. That girl sure knows how to accessorize.

"You like the Sox?" Connor asks.

"Of course," Cassandra says. "Big Sox fan."

"Really?" Connor smiles.

"Didn't you know that?" Cassandra takes her baseball hat off and flips her hair, which still looks perfect even after it was smooshed under a hat in the pouring rain. I touch my own hair, which feels damp and frizzy and completely icky.

Mr. Desmond jogs into class before Connor can answer. He shakes off his umbrella and hangs it on a coatrack in the corner of the classroom.

"Sorry I'm late, gang." He slips into the chair behind his desk. "It's a mess out there."

I pull out my notebook, but there's no way I can concentrate on science, so I stare at Cassandra. I know she's not really a Red Sox fan. Yesterday at lunch she admitted that she doesn't even like baseball. So is this all for Connor? I hear my pulse pounding in my ears. I can't believe she's such a faker. Does she really think Connor will ask her to the Spring Fling just because he thinks she likes baseball?

I shake off the feeling that Connor could actually like Cassandra and remember my promise to Mom and Dad— I'll keep up with my grades. I focus my attention on Mr. Desmond and the reproduction process of plants and plod through all my morning classes. I can't let myself be distracted by a boy. Especially a boy who might like Cassandra. Even if he is a super-sweet boy who likes baseball.

Cassandra and Katie are already eating by the time we get to lunch.

"Hey, Captain Obvious." Summer smiles at Cassandra.

"What's that supposed to mean?" Cassandra peers up at Summer through her Red Sox baseball cap.

"Oh, come on. We know why you're dressed like that."

"Yeah, because it's opening day. Duh." Cassandra takes off her cap and puts it on the empty seat next to her. Her hair *still* looks perfect.

"And you know about the Red Sox? Or anything about baseball?" Summer stabs her fork into a piece of pineapple.

"Of course not. But Connor doesn't need to know that." Cassandra raises her perfectly plucked eyebrows at Summer.

"I'm staying out of this." Summer pops the pineapple

into her mouth. "Hey, you guys have to see the dresses Bea made!"

"You make dresses?" Katie's eyes are as big as watermelons. "That's so cool."

"Bea's going to do a fashion show for Parents' Weekend. You want to model?"

"Well, we don't know that for sure—" I say.

"For real?" Katie interrupts. "We can be models?"

"Yeah, it's going to be awesome," Summer says. "So you'll do it?"

"Of course!" Katie says.

Cassandra jumps in with "I might do it too."

"What do you mean, you might? Didn't you hear me say it's going to be awesome?"

"I have to see the dresses first." Cassandra flips her hair.

"Believe me, they're incredible." Summer takes a bite of a strawberry. "Why don't we run up right now and you can take a look. We still have twenty minutes of break left."

"That sounds great," Katie says. "What about you, Cassandra?"

"I guess." Cassandra looks around the cafeteria. "Where's Connor anyway?"

Summer shrugs. Cassandra looks around the cafeteria again, rolls her eyes, and sighs. "Fine," she says. I guess since there's no sign of Connor it's safe for her to leave.

The rain cleared up, and Summer is jumping over puddles as she goes on and on about the dresses. My cheeks are burning, and I make sure to keep my head down as we walk so nobody can tell. I'm staring at the ground in front of me, which is how I happen to walk *right into* Connor.

"Yikes, I'm so sorry!" I try to smooth my hair down a bit.

"It's okay," Connor says. "I kind of snuck up on you guys."

"Hey, Connor." Cassandra jumps in front of me, and for once I'm grateful. This will give my face some time to go back to its normal color.

"Hi, Cassandra."

"Are you gonna watch the game tonight?" Cassandra takes her Red Sox hat off and shakes out her hair.

"Yeah. What do you think their chances are?" Connor asks.

"Whose chances for what?"

"The Sox. For winning."

"Oh, they'll totally win." Cassandra puts her hands on her hips.

"You think?"

"Of course. Why wouldn't they?"

"Well, you do know who they're playing." Connor raises his eyebrows.

Cassandra shifts her weight from one foot to the other. "Of course."

Connor nods. "Tough team. Especially with who's pitching."

Cassandra doesn't say anything.

"And you know, the Sox have a few guys—"

"Whatever. They'll totally win." Cassandra puts her hand on Connor's shoulder.

"You seem awfully sure." Connor tilts his head. "What do you think the score will be?

"What?" Cassandra's smile is unsteady.

"The score?" Connor raises his eyebrows. "Any predictions?"

Cassandra's face goes blank, until she blurts out, "Oh, you know, it will be high."

"Like thirty-two to forty-seven?" Connor asks, straight-faced. I purse my lips to stifle a giggle.

"Yeah, something like that." Cassandra stands up taller, smiling.

"Yeah, that's what I thought." Connor steps forward, and Cassandra's arm drops to her side. "Well, I gotta run. See you guys."

Summer laughs when Connor's out of earshot. "You're so funny, Cassandra. If you're going to fake like baseball, at least study a little!"

"What do you mean?" Cassandra tilts her head.

"Thirty-two to forty-seven? Baseball scores aren't that high." Summer laughs.

"I didn't think he'd really want to *talk* about it," Cassandra says, her hands flying up to put her cap back on.

Summer shakes her head, and I bite my lip to keep from smiling. Connor is too smart for Cassandra's games.

I knew there was a reason I liked him. Besides the dimples, I mean.

We get to our dorm room, and I pull the dresses out of my closet. I hand them to Summer, and she holds them up in front of her and prances around the room like a runway model.

"Wow, Bea." Katie takes one of the dresses out of Summer's hand. "These are amazing!"

"I told you!" Summer says.

"You actually *made* these?" Katie holds the dress at arm's length, looking it up and down.

"It's not that hard." I point to Ellie's sewing machine. "I use this."

"You know how to use a sewing machine?" Katie sounds amazed.

"Ell—" I stop myself and remember that nobody calls their grandmother by her first name. "My nana taught me."

Cassandra's holding up my silver dress, the one I wore to Sarriette's on my birthday. "This one's not bad."

"Not bad?" Summer stares at the dress. "It's incredible. I think it's my favorite."

"Okay, I'll be in your fashion show." Cassandra throws the dress on my bed. "We'd better go or we'll be late for language arts."

"We'll meet you there in a few." Summer picks up the silver dress Cassandra threw on the bed and hangs it up.

"Sometimes I wonder why I'm even friends with her," Summer says after Cassandra leaves.

"Why are you?" I'm glad she said something, because I was wondering about that myself.

"She wasn't always like this—she used to be really nice and fun. Now she's just selfish and fake. I know she's going through a rough year. Her parents are getting divorced so I try to give her a break."

"You're a good friend," I say. I can't imagine that Cassandra was ever nice. But then again, she's nowhere near as selfish and fake as Sophie was.

"Hey, you want to come to my house this weekend?" Summer asks on our way back to class.

I grin. "Sure, I'd love to—if you're sure it's okay."

"Of course it's okay." Summer jumps plop in the middle of a gigantic puddle. "Connor will probably come too."

"That's nice." My stomach does a little flip.

"Yeah, my parents like to have us home once in a while. And Connor loves coming to my house because my parents feed him well. Plus, he's got a huge man-crush on my dad."

I laugh. "A man-crush?"

"Yeah, you know—when a guy totally idolizes another guy? That's Connor with my dad."

I laugh again.

"It's fun for both of them," Summer says. "My dad only has daughters, so it's like Connor's his son. And Connor needs a father figure. Since his uncle's never around and all."

"Poor Connor," I say under my breath. I'm not even sure if Summer hears me.

"You're lucky you have your nana." Summer smiles at me. "Could you imagine what your life would have been like without her?"

"No," I say. And I mean it. I can't imagine my life without Ellie.

And then it hits me. Even though my parents aren't really dead, Connor and I do have something in common. We were both raised by people who aren't our parents. I know I can't compare us, not really. My parents love me, but sometimes I wonder if they love their careers just a little bit more.

# Chapter

## ★ 16 ★

HERE'S A KNOCK ON THE DOOR, AND MS. GOLDBERG peeks her head in.

"Hi, girls. Bea, this came for you." She hands me an envelope with the Midcoast Academy logo and address in the top left corner.

Summer runs over to me. "Open it, quick! It's probably about the Spotlight Project application."

My hands shake as I gently tear open the envelope and pull out the letter inside. Summer reads over my shoulder.

Dear Ms. Miller:

Congratulations! We are pleased to inform you that you have been selected as one of the finalists for Midcoast Academy's Parents' Weekend Spotlight Project.

The next step in the process is to set up an interview
with the selection committee.
Please be prepared to discuss your project in more detail.
Please check your school e-mail as your invitation
will be sent to you electronically.
Again, our congratulations, and I look forward to
meeting you soon.

Sincerely,
Betsy Banks
Selection Committee Chair

Summer screams and jumps up and down. "You're a finalist, Bea!"

I'm still standing there, holding the letter. I'm pretty sure my mouth is hanging open, but no words come out.

"Aren't you excited?" Summer's still jumping up and down.

"I—I just can't believe it."

"I told you! You're definitely going to win."

I run to my computer to check my e-mail. As promised, there's something in there about my interview. "They want to talk to me on Monday."

"Woo-hoo!" Summer jumps on her bed.

"But what will I say? I'm terrible at interviews." I slump in my chair.

"You'll do great. Just pretend you're talking to me."

I chuckle. "Maybe I can spray-paint the selection committee hot pink."

"Or, you can just picture them as hot pink people. That will relax you."

I don't realize, until this very minute, what the fashion show means to me. I squeeze my eyes shut and picture my friends walking the runway in my designs. My daydream is interrupted by Summer's groan.

"What's wrong?"

Summer slumps down in her desk chair. "I still have to study for the math test, and I hate math."

"But Mrs. Giraldi reviewed it in class."

Summer bites her lower lip and stares down at her book.

"Are you okay?" I ask her.

"I don't get it." Summer shakes her head.

"The math?"

"Yeah."

"Which part?"

"All of it."

I laugh, but for once Summer doesn't. She looks drop-dead serious.

"Want me to help?"

Summer looks up at me, and her eyes widen. "Can you?"

"Sure." I drag my desk chair next to hers and peek over her shoulder to the open math book.

"We have to find the radius of a circle." She says it like the words burn her tongue.

"That's easy!" I pull a sheet of paper out of her notebook. " I have to do this all the time when I'm making dresses."

"You mean you use math? In real life?" Summer raises one eyebrow.

"I guess I do." I shrug. Since it's so fun, I never thought of it as *math*. "First, we have to find your waist measurement."

I pull my measuring tape out of my desk drawer. Summer stands up, and I pull the tape tightly around her waist. "Twenty inches. So that would be the circumference."

I draw a circle on the piece of paper, as Summer looks over my shoulder.

"Ohhhhh," she squeals, then pokes her math book. "It says here that the formula for radius is circumference divided by pi, then divided by two."

"Yep, that's it. So if I measure the radius from the center of the circle, I'll know how much fabric I need." I draw this out on my paper, so she can see what I mean.

"I get it!" Summer bounces up and down. "It makes total sense when you explain it. Maybe you should be our math teacher."

I smile. Even I didn't realize I knew so much about math. Or maybe I just know a lot about sewing!

"Thanks, Bea." Summer grabs her pink fuzzy pencil and

writes furiously in her notebook. "You really helped me a lot."

"Are you kidding?" I laugh. "You're the one who helped me with all this Spotlight Project stuff."

"That's what friends are for." Summer flashes me a quick smile, then dives back into her math homework.

A burst of happiness bubbles from my stomach. I finally have a friend. A real friend.

But the bubbles pop when I remind myself that I'm still lying. And I'm suddenly scared, really scared. Because now I have so much to lose.

# Chapter
## ∗ 17 ∗

On FRIDAY AFTERNOON SUMMER AND I ROLL OUR suitcases out to the main entrance. Holly is already there, talking to Mrs. Kearney.

Summer parks her suitcase and plops down on the brown couch. "TGIF," she says with a smile.

Veronica and Eric open the front door. They chat with Mrs. Kearney and Holly for a few minutes. I look down the hall but don't see Connor. I wonder if he's still coming. Summer hurls herself off the couch and wheels her suitcase over to her parents.

"Can you take this?" she asks Eric. "I'm soooo tired."

Eric chuckles. "I think you can manage, kiddo."

"Mommy?" Summer hands her suitcase handle to Veronica.

"Your father says no so you ask me? I don't think so, munchkin."

"Fine," Summer sighs. "It was worth a try."

"Is Connor coming?" Veronica asks.

I hold my breath before Summer answers. "He should be."

Just as I exhale, Connor comes down the hall, a backpack strapped to his shoulders and something in his hand that I don't recognize.

"There he is," Eric says, and he and Connor shake hands. "Is that the sketch?"

"Yep, I think it's ready." Connor hands what looks like a rolled up poster to Summer's dad.

"Great, let's take a look when we get home." Eric pats Connor on the back, and Connor's dimples pop into full view.

"Have a great weekend," Mrs. Kearney says. "Oh, and Bea . . ."

I freeze. It takes me a few seconds to remember how to move my body, and I turn to look at her.

"I haven't yet heard back from your family about Parents' Weekend."

My hand is holding on to my suitcase handle so tight I think it might be stuck in a fist forever. Did she say "family" or "parents"? I think she said family. Family could mean anybody, right? Grandparents, aunts, cousins. So the fact that she said family won't seem too weird. I look around at the faces of Summer, Holly, and Connor. They're just staring at me, waiting for me to answer the question, so I take a deep breath and focus.

"Oh, yeah." I shift from one foot to the other. "I'm not sure yet, but I'll let you know."

"Okay, great." She holds the door open for us, and we all shuffle out, our suitcases making a steady rolling noise as we go.

Note to self: Be very careful around Mrs. Kearney.

"You guys actually drove?" Summer says as she eyeballs a Prius parked on the street.

"It looked like it might rain," Veronica says.

"My parents usually walk everywhere," Summer tells me.

"That's so cool," I say.

"You think so?" Summer slumps her shoulders. "Sometimes it gets tiring."

"We can't walk anywhere back home." We squeeze into Summer's car and load our suitcases in the back.

We drive for about three minutes, until we pull into the driveway of the cutest house I've ever seen. There are two rocking chairs on the front porch, which takes up half the front lawn. I take a deep breath when I get out of the car. The air smells like ocean, and when I turn around toward the backyard I see why. Half of the yard is a garden, and even though the flowers aren't out yet, the garden beds are clearly marked. The yard then continues to the bay, and a small dock juts out into the water. Two upside-down kayaks sit near the water's edge.

"C'mon." Summer skips to the front porch, rolling her suitcase behind her. A very excited yellow lab greets us as we open the door.

"Topaz!" Summer bends down, and Topaz immediately rolls over onto her back. Summer scratches the dog's belly and tells her how much she's missed her. Summer stands up and skips through the house, Topaz trotting after her.

"Let's go up to my room," Summer says. "I'll show you where to put your stuff."

Summer's room at home is practically identical to her room at school—an explosion of pink. There's a trundle bed already made up for me, complete with a hot pink fuzzy blanket. I drop my suitcase on the floor near the bed, and we make our way downstairs.

Connor and Eric are leaning over the kitchen table, the sketch Connor brought laid out in front of them. Veronica's sitting on the couch in the family room, her arm draped around Holly. They're looking at something in a magazine. Summer throws herself onto the couch, stretching her legs over Veronica's lap, and I sit down on a rocking chair. I'm amazed that I can see Connor and Eric from where I'm sitting. I can even hear every word they're saying—the rooms are *that* close to each other. I sink down into the chair as I realize the entire downstairs of Summer's house can probably fit in my bedroom. And yet, there's plenty of room for everyone. I feel warm and cozy—and included. I wonder if this is how a normal family is supposed to be, everyone home and hanging out. Together.

"Okay, gang." Veronica stands up. "Do we want pizza or Chinese?"

"Pizza!" Summer yells.

"Chinese," Holly says.

"We had Chinese last time." Summer sits up on the couch.

"Very true," Veronica says. "Is pizza okay with you, Bea?"

"Sure," I say. "I love pizza."

When the pizzas are delivered half an hour later—one plain, one veggie—Eric carries them into the family room and places them on top of the coffee table. Veronica puts a stack of plates next to them.

"Dig in," Eric says.

"Yes!" Summer fist-pumps the air. "I love Fridays. It's the one day in the week that we get to eat in the family room."

I've never eaten in our family room. Ellie and I usually eat at the kitchen counter when it's just the two of us. When my parents are home, we eat at the dining room table. Usually we have guests—my mom's agent or my dad's teammates—and dinner is all fancy. I can't remember the last time we ordered pizza, and suddenly I realize that's something we need to do more often.

Once everybody has a slice, Veronica turns on the TV. "Any suggestions?"

Summer turns to me. "Friday night is always take-out-and-TV night."

"That sounds fun." We're all sitting around the coffee table. Veronica and Eric are on one end of the couch, Holly's on the other. Connor is sitting on the floor, his back leaning against the couch, and Summer and I are each on a rocking chair.

Eric flips to the TV menu. "Sorry, Connor. No Sox game tonight."

"Who's playing?" Connor asks.

"Let's see." Eric scans the menu. "Yankees and Phillies."

Connor groans. A true Red Sox fan.

"How about the Dodgers and Cubs?"

"That could be a good game," Connor says. "Who's pitching?"

Eric flips to the game, and I almost choke on my pizza.

"Are you okay, Bea?" Veronica jumps off the couch. "Let me get you some water."

"I'm—I'm okay," I manage to say in between coughing fits. I try to cover my face with my hair so nobody—especially Connor—can see how red I am.

Veronica hands me a glass of water, and I gulp it down. "Thank you," I manage.

"Is the pizza too cheesy?" Summer asks.

"No, I just swallowed wrong." I take another gulp of water.

Now that I'm no longer choking, the attention turns back to the TV, which is still playing the Dodgers game.

"Is Zack Miller pitching?" Eric asks.

"I hope so," Veronica begins. "He's nice to look at."

I practically pour water down my throat to keep from gagging.

*Please, please, please, Dad, don't be pitching tonight,* I silently beg. *Please please please.* I absolutely cannot watch my dad on TV right now without losing it.

"No, Roberto Sanchez is pitching," Connor says. "He's not that good."

I'm so grateful to Connor I could hug him. Well, almost.

"How about a movie instead?" Veronica asks.

"That sounds great!" I say just a little too loudly.

We settle in for a movie. It's one of those lighthearted family-friendly flicks. When it's over, Summer and I stand and stretch. Luckily, I have the weekend off from Face-Time. I told my parents that Summer's family doesn't have a good Internet connection. I know I should feel bad about lying to them, but that's the smallest lie of all the lies I've told, so I shake it off. I promised I'd text instead, but that's easy—I could do it from under the covers.

Connor will sleep in Eric's office, which has a futon in it. They're in there now, talking about the sketch.

"What is that sketch for?" I ask Summer.

"Only the coolest thing ever." She grabs my hand and marches me into Eric's office. "It's the sketch for the observation deck, the one Connor's going to build off the science room? Isn't it pure awesomeness?"

I look over her shoulder at what I assume is a photo of a deck with benches around the edges. "That's a really nice one. Where is it?"

Connor's dimples get even deeper. "Nowhere. At least not yet. It's the drawing for the observation deck we're going to put in at Midcoast."

"You *drew* that?" I squint to get a better look.

"Yep." He unrolls the paper to reveal the full sketch of the deck, complete with a telescope tucked into the corner. But that's not the best part. The best part is the picture of the sky.

"That's amazing." I stare at the sketch. "That sky looks so real."

"Did you see many stars back home?"

I'm about to say that I have seen a lot, until I realize that he's talking about the kind in the sky, not the kind in Hollywood.

"Not really." I play with my ruby necklace.

Connor nods. "That's probably because of the light

pollution in Southern California. It's one of the things I love most about Maine. You can see the stars."

"I noticed that as soon as I got here. It looks like someone punched a bazillion holes in the sky."

Connor pulls out his sketchbook. "It's amazing what a difference the light pollution makes. This is a picture of the sky in Boston." He flips to a drawing of the night sky, which looks like he lay down in the middle of a city and started drawing. I can see the tops of buildings, and only a few stars sprinkled throughout.

Connor flips the page. "And this is a picture of the sky in Maine." He must have drawn this from the same angle, but instead of buildings I see treetops, and more stars than I've ever seen before. I'm not sure how he made it look this way, because the picture is drawn in pencil. But it's so real I swear I'm looking at a photo.

My mouth is hanging open, and I realize I haven't said anything for the last minute. I'm just staring at Connor's sketch, and he's staring at me. Probably waiting for me to talk. Which I can't, because how can I tell him that this is the most beautiful thing I've ever seen without sounding like I've got a gigantic crush on him?

"It's really good." That's the best I can come up with.

"Thanks. I thought it would be cool to have a place at Midcoast where everyone can not only learn about the stars, but also spend time really looking at them."

"What's this?" I point to a rectangular shape attached to the center railing of the deck.

"Oh." Connor looks at me, but his dimples—and his smile—are gone. "That's the dedication."

I remember Connor telling me he's dedicating the observation deck to his parents. Nobody says anything for a few seconds, and then Summer chimes in. "Connor and Dad are going to build it all summer. The school's right behind it."

"Wow," I say.

"Yeah." Summer nods. "It's way cooler than pond scum."

"I heard that!" Holly yells from the other room.

After some more oohing and aahing over Connor's sketches, Eric ushers us upstairs so we can get ready to go to sleep.

Summer and I are in bed giggling when Veronica comes in. "Ready for lights-out?"

"Can't we stay up just a little bit later?" Summer asks.

"Tell you what," Veronica says. "I'll tuck you in now, but you can talk for a little while longer."

"Deal!" Summer nods.

Veronica pulls our blankets up, gives each of us a kiss on the cheek, and turns off the light. "Good night, girls."

"Does your mom always tuck you in?" I ask after Veronica leaves.

"Of course." Summer pauses. "It must be really hard, not having a mom to tuck you in."

"Yeah," I agree. "It is."

Only Summer doesn't know that I do have a mom. But she doesn't tuck me in much. She used to, when I was a little girl, and she wasn't such a big star. Now, even when she is home, she spends her nights at tapings or at fancy dinners with network bigwigs.

"So, have you thought any more about what kinds of dresses you're going to make?" Summer flips her pillow over.

"Not yet," I say. "I'm trying not to get too excited, you know, in case I don't win."

"You'll totally win. Your project's awesomesauce."

I stare at the ceiling. "How come Connor isn't applying for the Project Spotlight with his observation deck?"

Even though the room is dark, I can see Summer shrug.

"It's a really cool project. Connor and your dad are going to build that whole thing themselves?"

"Yep."

"With what?"

"With tools." She says this as if it's perfectly normal. As if people build their own stuff all the time. "My dad built this house."

"*This* house? The one we're in now?"

"Yep."

"That's amazing. I've never heard of anyone building a house."

Summer laughs. "Doesn't anyone build things in California?"

"Not anyone I know," I admit.

"What's it like, where you live in California?"

"It's nice I guess. I like my house, but it's too big for us."

"Really? Wow!"

I bite my lower lip. For a second I forgot that Summer doesn't know about my real life. "Uhhh, yeah. It's pretty big."

"Do you have a pool?"

"Yes. And a hot tub."

"Awesome!" Summer flips her pillow again. "Maybe we can come visit during summer break.

I blink. I can't believe Summer wants to visit me. Me. Not my parents. There's a tug at my stomach, and more than ever I want to tell Summer the truth about me. I want her to know who I really am.

"Hey, Summer . . ."

"Yeah?"

"I have something to tell you."

# Chapter
## ⋆18⋆

MY PHONE BUZZES JUST AS I'M ABOUT TO BLAB. I grab it off the nightstand. It's a text from my mom.

"Who's texting so late?" Summer peers over the covers.

I take a deep breath in. I should tell her. I was just going to tell her anyway, but the text has jerked me back to reality, and I realize this isn't the right time. What if she's mad at me and won't speak to me? What if she kicks me out of her house?

"It's my nana. Just checking in." I shoot a quick response off to my mom, and put the phone back on the nightstand.

"So, what'd you want to tell me?" Summer asks.

"Just that I really appreciate you inviting me to your house." Which is totally true.

"Of course! You can come anytime." Summer yawns and turns over. "G'night, Bea."

"Good night, Summer."

In a few minutes I can hear Summer's slow and steady breathing. I'm always amazed at how fast she falls asleep. I stare at the ceiling for what seems like hours, trying to think of a good way—and time—to tell Summer the truth about myself.

The house is dark, so I figure everyone's asleep. I push the covers off and get out of bed as quietly as I can. My mouth feels like it's stuffed with cotton balls, so I tiptoe downstairs to get something to drink. I take a glass from the cupboard, fill it with water, and creep through the kitchen past Eric's office (where Connor is sleeping!) to the foot of the stairs.

"Bea?" It's Connor's voice.

I jump. "Oh, sorry. I was just getting some water. Did I wake you?"

"No." He stretches. "Can't sleep."

"Me neither."

I look down at my water. "Summer's house is really nice."

Even though it's dark, I can see Connor's eyes light up. "I know, right? Did you see all the skylights?"

"Oh, uh, I didn't really notice that."

"Oh, you've got to see one."

I follow him into the kitchen. The lights are out, and I can barely see him in front of me. He stops underneath a skylight, and I stop inches from him. He looks up.

"See?"

"Wow." It was amazing how many stars we can see through the skylight.

"Can you see the Big Dipper?"

I squint. "I don't know what to look for."

"It looks like a sideways question mark." He points up through the glass.

"I just see globs of stars."

"Look at the lower right-hand corner of the skylight. The stars in the Big Dipper are pretty bright."

I shift my gaze to where he tells me and cock my head to the side. Just as I'm about to give up, I spot something that does, in fact, look like a sideways question mark. "I see it!"

"That's the Big Dipper."

"Cool."

"Yeah, it is." He nods.

We stare in silence for about a minute. I can't think of anything to say, so I blurt the first thing that comes to my mind.

"Hey, did you hear about the Sox game?"

"You like the Sox?" Connor sounds skeptical. I can't really blame him after Cassandra's ridiculousness.

"Not really." I shrug. "But I love baseball. I'm a huge Dodgers fan."

"For real?" Connor's teeth are white in the darkness.

"Totally," I say. And then I wish I hadn't. Because I know what's coming next.

"You should have said something sooner. We could have watched the game tonight."

"Oh, no, that's okay. I don't need to watch every game." I wave my hand in front of my face like it's no big deal.

"Who's your favorite player?"

Silence.

I purse my lips and look up like I'm thinking. "Billy Sanders."

"He's a great shortstop."

"Yeah. With a three-thirteen batting average." I nod. He's also an awesome cook and tells great jokes. But I don't mention those things.

I don't want him to ask me any more questions about the Dodgers, and I don't know what else to talk about, so I turn around and head up the stairs. "Good night." I give him a wave.

"Good night." He steps back into Eric's office and closes the door.

I crawl into bed and tug the covers over my face. When will I ever learn to talk to boys without sounding like a total idiot?

I don't know when I finally fall asleep, but I wake up to bright sunshine and Topaz licking my face.

"Hi, girl." I wipe dog drool off my chin. Summer sits up in her bed and rubs her eyes, which widen at the sight of her dog.

"Down, Topaz!" She points to the floor, and Topaz jumps off the bed. "I'm sorry. Did she wake you up?"

"That's okay," I say. "She's so sweet." Topaz is standing at the floor by my bed wagging her tail.

"Since we're up, let's go get breakfast." Summer springs out of bed, which excites Topaz to no end. I push the blankets off of me and stretch my arms above my head. I slowly get out of bed, stretch again, and throw a sweatshirt on over my pajamas. Summer bounces down the stairs ahead of me. She's always perky in the morning.

Yummy breakfast smells waft from the kitchen, and my nose immediately identifies French toast and coffee. The smell of coffee reminds me of breakfast at my house, which I usually ate alone at the kitchen counter. When I get into the kitchen, Eric is putting French toast on a big platter, Veronica's cutting up fruit, and Connor's setting the table.

"Good morning, sleepyheads," Veronica greets us cheerfully. "Breakfast is ready."

"Cool!" Summer fist-pumps the air. "And we didn't even have to do any of the work."

"Don't worry," Eric says. "You can clean up."

"Awwww." Summer's lower lip juts out.

"We wouldn't want you to miss out on any of the fun." Eric winks.

We all sit down and dig in. Topaz sits right next to Summer, on alert for anything that might fall off her plate.

This is exactly what I imagined normal families to be like. As much as I love my parents and I know they love me, we just don't spend time together like this.

At breakfast we don't talk about television ratings, or which Hollywood star got plastic surgery. We talk about school. We talk about the weather. We talk about Parents' Weekend, which is fun now that I know my parents aren't coming.

"Summer tells us you'll be doing a fashion show for the Spotlight Project," Veronica says.

I can feel my ears heat up. "Well, maybe. If I win."

"She'll win." Summer takes a gulp of orange juice.

"You applied for the Spotlight Project?" Connor asks. I look up from my plate. Everyone's staring at me.

"Yeah, but it's not a big deal, really, I just—Summer thought—"

"It *is* a big deal," Summer squeals. "You guys have to see Bea's dresses. She makes them herself. With a real sewing machine. We're going to have a fashion show and model them, so everyone can see how awesome they are."

"How exciting," Veronica says. "I can't wait to see it."

I'm very happy when the conversation shifts from my fashion show to Connor's observation deck.

"So if we break ground at the beginning of June," Connor says, "we should be finished by the time school starts again."

Eric nods. "That's the plan."

"What a talented group of kids we have here." Veronica pours herself some coffee. It smells really good, but for the first time in a long time, I don't want any. It's really nice to be a regular kid.

"Okay, kiddo." Eric leans back in his chair and smiles at Summer. "You can clear the table."

"Gee, thanks," Summer says.

"I'll help you." I pick up my plate and walk around the table to gather the others.

"You don't have to, Bea. It's my chore."

"I want to," I say, and I mean it. One, because I want to help Summer, and two, because I'll do anything to live like a normal kid, including doing dishes. I've never cleaned up after a meal before, but I've watched Ellie a million times, so I know what to do.

I clear the table, and Summer loads the dishwasher. Once I wipe the table off, Connor and Eric unroll the sketch and huddle around it.

"It's almost time to leave for the dentist," Veronica yells down from upstairs.

"Ugh, I forgot about that." Summer pours the soap in the dishwasher and presses start.

"Mom's taking me and Holly. Want to stay here with Connor and my dad?"

I glance up at Connor, who glances up at me at the exact same time. "Sure, I guess." I shrug.

Since I'm not sure what else I should do, I stand next to Connor and look down at the sketch sprawled across the kitchen table. "You did all this yourself?"

"Nah." Connor shakes his head. "Eric helped me."

"Hardly," Eric says. "I only helped get everything to scale. Connor did the real work."

Just as I'm about to tell them how amazing it is, the phone rings. Eric runs into the office to answer it, so Connor and I are left standing at the kitchen table. Alone. Again. I say a silent prayer that I'll think of something brilliant to say.

Nothing comes to me.

"That's really cool," Connor says. "About your fashion show."

"Thanks, but it's not nearly as cool as your observation deck. You should have applied for the Spotlight Project."

"Nah," Connor says. "It's not anywhere near ready yet."

"Even what you have is amazing."

"Do you sketch your stuff out first?" Connor asks.

"Mm-hm." I nod, hoping my face isn't as red as it feels.

"I've never met anyone else who carries a sketchbook around."

"Me neither!" I say this a little too enthusiastically, but I'm thrilled that Connor and I have another thing in common. A real thing.

"Can I see your sketches?" Connor asks.

"Oh, you don't have to—"

"I want to." Connor gives me a smile.

"Okay. I'll be right back." I dart up the stairs and pull my sketchpad out of my suitcase. Connor's sitting at the kitchen table when I get back. Eric is still on the phone.

Connor rolls up his sketch, and I place my sketchpad on the table in front of him. My heart is beating a trillion miles a minute. I'm not sure if that's because I flew down the stairs or if it's because Connor is looking at my work.

He goes to open the pad, and I instinctively plop my hand on top of it.

"What?" He laughs.

"It's just…" I sigh. "Nobody's ever seen my sketches before."

"Nobody?" He raises his eyebrows.

"No," I say. "I just never thought to show anyone."

"Yeah," he says. "I never showed anyone my stuff either till I met Eric."

"Really?" I ask. "But it's so good."

Connor shrugs. "I guess I just didn't think anyone would care about a bunch of drawings."

"That's exactly how I feel." I'm nodding my head so hard I get dizzy. "I mean, who cares about a bunch of stupid dresses that I draw?"

"I do," Connor says in a small voice.

Now my heart is beating so fast that I'm pretty sure it's going to hurl itself out of my body and land right on top of the table. I take a deep breath and move my hand off of the sketchpad as Connor flips to the first page.

# Chapter
## ★ 19 ★

HIS EYES WIDEN WHEN HE LOOKS AT THE FIRST sketch. I hold my breath.

"This is awesome," he says.

"You don't have to say that. You won't hurt my feelings if you—"

"No, I'm serious." He flips through the pages, looking carefully at the rest of the designs. "You're really talented."

There's that word again. And Connor is using it to describe *me*. I realize my mouth is hanging open, so I close it before he looks up at me.

"Thank you," I say, my smile a mile wide.

"These are great. You should be a fashion designer someday." Connor smiles. "But I bet you already thought of that."

"Not really," I say. "I never really thought about what I wanted to do when I grew up. I mean, I love designing clothes, but I just figured I'd never be good enough."

"Are you kidding me? You're probably good enough already."

A rush of warmth floods my entire body, and it takes all of my self-control to keep my feet glued to the ground. I just want to scream and yell and jump up and down.

Connor is still looking at the sketches, spending several minutes on each one. "Seems that's another thing we have in common. We both like to sketch."

"Do you have more drawings?" I ask.

"Tons."

"Can I see them?"

"I guess that's only fair."

I follow Connor out to the patio. His sketchbook is on the table. The silver design on the cover catches the sun so it looks like the book is covered in starlight. He opens it up and flips to the first page. It's a perfect drawing of Summer's house at night.

"That's amazing." I stare at the sketch. "It looks exactly like Summer's house. Exactly."

"I hope so." Connor laughs. "I was in the front yard when I drew it."

"The stars look so real."

He flips the page and I recognize the next drawing

immediately. It's the main office at Midcoast Academy. Again, at night.

"You even drew the porch swing. That really makes the building come to life. Do you always draw pictures at night?" I force my eyes away from the drawing so I can look at him. He's still looking at the sketch.

"Yep. The buildings and stuff are just background. The stars are what I really want to show. It's cool to be able to change the constellations around however I want. It's like being the controller of the universe." He laughs. "Well, at least controller of my sketchpad."

He turns the page again. There's another sketch of a house at night, but this one I don't recognize.

"This is the house I lived in till my parents died," he says quietly.

"Oh wow." I stare at the sketch. "Did you draw that from memory?"

"No, my uncle had a picture of it."

"It's really amazing," I say. "It looks so much like a photo."

"I look at this sketch every night before I go to sleep, hoping I'll remember something about living there."

"Do you?" My eyes focus on Connor's face, but he's focused on the sketch.

"No," he says. "No matter how hard I try."

"It's a really nice house," I say.

"Yeah." Connor laughs, but it's not a funny kind of laugh. "I just wish I remembered living there."

I look down at the drawing and nod.

"Don't you wish you could remember more?" Connor looks at me. I look down at the table.

"I guess," I say, my brain searching for ways to politely change the subject without seeming too insensitive. I really don't want to give fake answers to his questions.

"You don't like to talk about it much, huh?" Connor leans back in his chair, and I squirm in mine.

"I guess not," I say. "I don't want to think too much about bad stuff that happened in the past. Especially when so much good stuff is happening now."

Connor breaks out into a huge smile. "You're right. Sometimes I know I think too much about them—about the past."

"You should totally think about them," I say. "You should always remember them and what they meant to you. But you have to live your life, too, you know?"

"Yeah, thanks. It's really nice to get advice from someone who understands."

And there's that old familiar yank on my stomach. The yank that tells me what a bad person I am, lying to Connor, to Summer, to Summer's incredibly nice family. Suddenly I feel sick because what I'm doing is so awful.

"Hey, you wanna take the kayak out?" Connor pushes his chair back and stands up.

"I—uhhh—are we allowed?" I stammer.

"Yeah, as long as we wear life jackets. Let me go grab a couple and let Eric know what we're doing."

"Okay." I stand up and walk over to the dock. I've never been in a kayak before, and I wonder if I'll wind up falling out—right in front of Connor. My cheeks burn just thinking about how completely lame that would be.

Connor jogs toward me with two life jackets in his hands and Topaz barking behind him.

"You have to stay, Topaz. We'll be back soon." He gives the dog a pat on the head and flips one of the kayaks over. I breathe a little easier when I see it's a two-person boat. At least I won't have to pilot my own. Pilot? I wonder if that's even the right word to use for a boat driver.

Connor drags the kayak until it's next to the dock. We put on our life jackets, and he holds the back of the boat. "Climb in."

I start to put my right foot in, when Connor laughs. "You've never been in a kayak?"

I nod, mortified that it's so obvious.

"You should get down low. You don't want to get in while standing. It's a little tippy."

Tippy. Great.

I do as he says and practically crawl into the boat. Once

I'm finally in, he hands me a paddle. Then he effortlessly slides himself down onto his seat, behind mine, and pushes us off the dock.

"Whoa!" I yell, as we glide through the water. The boat is rocking back and forth like a baby's cradle.

"See? Tippy," Connor says.

I make a sound that's half whimper, half screech.

"Need a lesson?" Connor asks.

"Is it that bad?"

"Only because you're holding the paddle, but you aren't exactly paddling."

I am so very grateful that he's behind me and can't see that my face is redder than it's ever been in my whole entire life.

"Here," he says. "Let me show you."

I turn around and watch as he paddles, left then right. "Looks easy enough."

"It is easy. Give it a try."

I gently dip my paddle in the water, copying his movements.

"You got it!" He laughs. "Don't they have boats in California?"

I don't tell him about the boats that I go on. I figure mentioning the two-hundred-foot yachts and million-dollar cruisers might raise a few unwanted questions. "Kayaking is new to me."

We paddle out to the middle of the bay until the only sound I can hear is our paddles hitting the water. Otherwise, it's totally silent.

"This is so nice," I say.

"Yeah." Connor picks his paddle out of the water and I do the same, so we gently drift along in the water. "This is my favorite place on earth."

"I can see why."

"Someday I'll build a house on the bay," Connor says. "I'll be an astronomer, and I'll paddle out every night when the sun sets and watch the stars. Oh, and I'll have a dog like Topaz."

Although Connor can't see me, I smile a big dippy smile. It's nice hearing him talk about his dreams. I wish that we weren't on a boat so I could turn around and hug him. Most of all, I wish I weren't so dorky around boys.

"I think that's a good plan" is what I say instead. "And I'll be a fashion designer. I'll make clothes for kids like Summer who aren't afraid to be unique."

"Summer can be your head salesperson," Connor says.

"That's a great idea!" The boat swishes back and forth. "We can base our business in town and sell to all the kids at Midcoast."

"So you'd like to stay here in Maine?" Connor asks.

I shrug. "I've never thought about that."

"Do you miss California?"

"No," I say, without missing a beat. "Not at all, actually. Except Ellie—I mean, my nana. I miss her."

"Maybe she could move here," Connor says.

I laugh. "She hates the cold."

"Hey," Connor says. "Can I ask you a serious question?"

I turn my head to look at him. "Sure."

Connor looks down at the paddle on his lap. "Would you— Will you go to the Spring Fling with me?"

# Chapter
## ★20★

I DROP MY PADDLE. IT MAKES A *SPLOOSH* SOUND AS IT lands in the water.

*"Omigod!"* I reach for it, but as I do so, the boat wobbles like crazy.

"It's okay," Connor says. "Just stay still. If you lean over like that the boat will tip."

Who cares about the boat tipping? Connor just asked me to the Spring Fling! I suddenly feel like I just chugged a gallon of coffee.

Connor steers us over to the floating paddle. He carefully slides it over to the kayak with his paddle, and then lifts it out of the water.

"Here you go." He slides the paddle over to me, and I grab it, droplets of water falling onto my lap.

"I am so sorry. It's just that—you surprised me."

"Surprised good or surprised bad?"

"Surprised good." I am so so so glad he can't see my face right now. I'm sure the back of my hair looks horrible given that there are droplets of water all over it, but it's got to be less embarrassing than my bright red cheeks.

"Does that mean you'll go with me?"

"Uhhhh. Yes." I keep a death grip on the paddle.

Neither of us say another word, and my heartbeat is almost normal by the time we paddle back to Summer's house. Eric has lemonade waiting, and the three of us drink it on the patio. Connor and Eric unroll the sketch.

"What do you think about these benches?" Connor's looking at me instead of Eric.

"Me?" I look behind me to be sure nobody else is there.

"Yeah. You're good with design."

I lean forward and find the spot he's pointing at. "They're nice, but I think they should be curved a little. They'd look more natural that way, especially since they're outside."

"You know, you're right," Eric says. "If we look at the design of the dome, and the tree line, everything is rounded a bit. Good call, Bea."

I instantly sit up straighter. I'm so busy talking with Connor and Eric about the sketch that I don't hear the car pull up. Summer skips into the backyard holding a small plastic bag with a picture of a big tooth.

"What's going on?" she says when she sees us huddled around the patio table. "Don't tell me they've got you sucked into this too, Bea?"

"Are you kidding?" Connor smiles. "Bea's given us some great ideas. She knows a lot about design stuff."

"Duh." Summer rolls her eyes. "I've been saying that for days now."

I wonder if Summer knows that Connor asked me to the Spring Fling. I try to tell her with my eyes while motioning my head toward Connor, but she's just squinting at me, and I realize I must look like a demented owl.

"I'm hungry." Summer opens the door that leads into the house. "Anyone want some grapes?"

"I do!" I say, way too enthusiastically. "I'll come with you."

I follow Summer into the kitchen. "You're not going to believe what happened!"

"Connor asked you to the Spring Fling?" Summer opens the refrigerator door and pulls out a bowl of grapes.

"How did you know?" I gasp.

"He told me he was going to." Summer bites a grape in half.

"He told you?" I put my hands on my hips. "And you didn't tell me?"

"He asked me not to. I figured you'd find out soon enough anyway." Summer giggles.

"Eeeeek," I squeak. "What will I wear?"

"Ohhhh, you can design a special dress—a Spring Fling dress! I have some amazing ideas."

"You do? Let's get started sketching it!"

I grab the sketchpad off the kitchen table, and we run up to Summer's room. We put the sketchpad in the middle of the floor and start spewing ideas at each other.

"It should have flowers at the hem," Summer says.

"Definitely sleeveless," I say.

More than anything, I want to win the Spotlight Project. Nobody's ever believed in my designs like Summer does, and I want to prove to her that she's right. I want to prove it to myself, too.

For the first time in my life, I think maybe, just maybe, I have a sprinkle of talent somewhere inside of me. And this will be the first chance I've ever had to let it out.

# Chapter
## ★ 21 ★

I GO TO THE MAIN OFFICE ON MONDAY AT THREE O'CLOCK, the time of my interview. Mrs. Kearney brings me to a room that I've never been to before. It's got a long table with twelve cushy chairs around it. There are six people in the chairs, and they all look up when I walk in.

"You must be Bea." The lady sitting nearest to the door stands up and shakes my hand. "I'm Mrs. Banks."

"Nice to meet you," I say. I can't quite meet her eyes, so I stare at her starfish necklace.

"Please, sit down." Mrs. Banks motions me to sit in one of the cushy chairs. All of the other adults have folders and notepads opened in front of them, and all eyes are on me.

I scoot back in the chair, to be sure I'm sitting up straight, but the chair swivels and I let out a little squeal. Mrs. Banks smiles at me. Either she didn't hear me, or she's pretending she didn't.

"So, Bea." Mrs. Banks flips through my application. "You like to design dresses?"

"Yes." I nod and gently push my portfolio toward her. "Here are some of my sketches, if you'd like to see them."

"Oh, thank you." Mrs. Banks puts her glasses on and flips through the pages.

"Oh my." Mrs. Banks raises her eyebrows, and I sink into my chair.

She hates them. Of course she hates them. I am lame, just like Sophie said. Lame and talentless. I look at where I'm sitting. I look at the door, wondering if I can slink out of here without anyone noticing.

Then I remember what Summer thinks. And what Connor said. And I glance across the table to see what Mrs. Banks is looking at. My stuff is good. I'm not talentless. Sophie was wrong and mean and awful. I sit up a little straighter, folding my hands in my lap.

After looking at most of the pages, Mrs. Banks passes the book to the woman on her right. She whispers something, but I can't hear what it is. My heart starts racing.

"Bea." Mrs. Banks takes off her glasses. "Have you had any formal training?"

"Formal training?" My voice sounds like it's coming from somewhere outside my body.

"Yes. Have you ever taken any design classes?"

"No." The back of my neck feels sweaty.

The woman to the right of Mrs. Banks slides the book to the man on her right. She doesn't say anything at all.

"I see," says Mrs. Banks. "May I see your sample?"

"My what?" At this point her words are muffled sounds without meaning.

"I assume that's one of your dresses that you're holding?" Her eyes shoot to my lap.

"Oh." I hold up the dress. I completely forgot I even had it. "Yes, this is a sample." It's a sky-blue sleeveless back-zip A-line with a gathered empire waist. I've actually never worn it, but I've always thought it was pretty.

"Is it okay if we take a look?" Mrs. Banks nods, prodding me to hand the dress over.

"Oh, sure." I hand her the dress, but she doesn't smile, or say thank you, or anything. She just looks at the dress from every angle possible. She even turns it inside out.

"Who taught you how to sew?"

"My nanny. Nana. Grandmother." I stutter over the words.

Mrs. Banks just nods. "Do you mind if we hold on to this? Until we make a decision? Then we'll give everything back to you."

"Sure, that would be fine." I try to smile, but my cheeks are frozen with nerves.

"Thank you for coming today, Bea." I think Mrs. Banks smiles, but she might just have a twitch.

"Oh, okay." I look at the door. "So is that it?"

"Yes, dear. You can go now." Mrs. Banks slides out of her chair and walks me to the door. "Thanks again. It was a pleasure meeting you."

"Thank you." She has her hand on my back, but that may be because she's trying to push me out of the room.

The door closes behind me, and I slide down the hallway wall into a heap on the floor.

I don't know how I let Summer talk me into this. Sure, I love my designs. And so do some of my other friends, but what if Mrs. Banks hates them?

I pull myself up off the floor and drag myself back to my dorm. Summer's not going to be happy about this.

# Chapter

## ★ 22 ★

ALL I CAN THINK ABOUT FOR THE NEXT FEW DAYS IS how awful that interview was. I try to tell Summer that I stunk up the place, but she seems unfazed. She's still planning the fashion show, recruiting models, and acting like her usual happy self.

I just walk around in a zombielike state. I can't believe I let myself get my hopes up.

Summer and I are doing homework—well, Summer's doing homework and I'm staring at a blank screen—when there's a knock on the door.

"Come in!" Summer yells.

"Hi, girls," Ms. Goldberg says. "Special delivery."

Summer leaps off her chair as Ms. Goldberg hands me another envelope with the Midcoast logo.

"Omigod, omigod, omigod, omigod. That's it, Bea. Open it!" Summer's jumping all over the room.

"Okay, but don't get too excited. I told you the interview was horrible." I squeeze the envelope to my chest.

"Just open it! I can't stand the suspense." Summer's waving her hands in front of her chest so hard I think she might be vibrating.

I take a deep breath and open the envelope.

I slowly unfold the letter.

Dear Ms. Miller:

On behalf of the Spotlight Project Selection Committee, I am happy to inform you that you are the winner of this year's Spotlight Project.

Your application to produce a fashion show on Saturday, May 19, has been approved. Please provide all final plans to me no later than April 24.

Attached please find a check in the amount of $100.00. Congratulations, and I look forward to a special event!

Sincerely,
Betsy Banks
Selection Committee Chair

And then, in flawless handwriting, a note that reads:

*Your dresses are exquisite! I look forward to the day that I'll be able to wear one of your designs.*

"You won! You won! You won!" Summer's dancing around the room. "I told you you would."

"Do you think they made a mistake?" I'm staring at the letter.

"No, goofy! You won. Now do you believe me that your dresses are fantastical?"

I don't know what to believe. I'm too stunned to talk. I'm too stunned to even breathe.

"We've got work to do." Summer claps her hands together and opens her computer. "Let's get started."

As I go to sit next to her, my first instinct is to call Ellie and my parents and tell them. But if I tell them, they'll definitely come to Parents' Weekend. To my fashion show.

*My* fashion show. If my parents attended, nothing would be *mine* anymore. The fashion show wouldn't be about me. It would be about the daughter of Zack Miller and Celestine Cruz. Nobody would come to the fashion show to see my designs, they'd come to get a glimpse of my parents. My designs—and me—would be invisible. Or worse, I'd be compared to my parents. Sophie's words ring in my brain. *How can you have a star baseball player as a dad and a supermodel as a mom and be so—talentless?*

"Hello?" Summer pats the chair next to her. "What are you waiting for?"

I slide into the chair and brush the thought of my parents aside. This is a special moment for me, I decide. And I can't let anything ruin it. I can worry about my parents later.

But not yet.

# Chapter

## ★ 23 ★

$\mathcal{D}$ONE!" I PUT THE LAST STITCH IN SUMMER'S T-SHIRT dress and hold it up for her to see.

"Whoa." Summer throws the book she was reading onto her bed and leaps over to me. "It looks even better than I thought it would."

"Really?" I hand her the dress, which she holds like a carton of eggs. "Go try it on."

She carefully carries the dress to her side of the room, throws off her old clothes, and slips into her new design.

"This. Is. Amazing." She twirls around and around, and the hem of the skirt poofs up. I designed it that way on purpose, since I know how much Summer likes to spin. And spin. And spin.

"It looks so good on you." I can't wipe the smile off my

face. Nobody but me has ever worn one of my dresses before.

"I am *so* excited to wear this. Wait till everybody sees it, Bea! You'll have orders coming in by the truckload!"

We hear a bunch of kids in the hallway, which means it's dinnertime.

"I should have Katie's dress done by next week, and Cassandra's done the week after that." We follow the other kids to the cafeteria.

"I can't believe Parents' Weekend is only three weeks away," Summer says.

"I can't believe it either."

Summer opens her mouth to say something but closes it before words come out. Instead, she gives me a weak smile, and I know she's thinking about my lack of parents. I try to smile back.

Cassandra and Katie are already at the table when we get to the cafeteria. Katie squeals when she sees Summer's dress and begs me to make one for her.

Cassandra is decked out in a bright yellow eyelet sundress and matching strappy sandals. I think it's a little cool to be wearing a sundress, even if it does have a fabulous circular hem, but at least she stopped wearing Red Sox gear. Summer's telling them about their dresses for the fashion show, and Katie looks mesmerized. Cassandra looks bored.

"Here comes Connor." Cassandra fluffs her hair. "How do I look?"

"Great!" I say a little too loudly. Cassandra raises her eyebrows at me, a sideways smile plastered on her face. I sink a little lower into my chair. I still haven't told her that Connor asked me to the Spring Fling. It's not like I stole Connor from her or anything. He never even liked her in the first place. And anyway, Cassandra's never been nice to me. I shouldn't feel bad. I know I shouldn't. But I still do.

Connor, Shane, and a boy named Timmy who I've only met a couple of times carry their trays over to our table. There's an empty seat next to me. Shane elbows Connor and sits down in the seat farthest away, forcing Connor to sit next to me. If I sink any lower in my chair I'll be on the floor. I try anyway.

"Hi, guys." Cassandra looks directly at Connor.

They all mumble some sort of greeting. Timmy starts talking, but I can barely understand what about—words are flying out of his mouth at the speed of light. Connor and Shane are cracking up, so they must know what he's saying. Maybe it's a secret boy language.

"How's the chocolate cake?" Connor points to my tray. Timmy is still talking.

I pick up the dish and hold it out. "Want some?"

He picks up his fork and stabs at the cake. Cassandra

is staring at him, and she looks like he just bit the head off a puppy.

"Awww, the love birds are sharing food." Well, Timmy sure said *that* clearly enough.

I put my head down and will my hair to fall in my face. I peer at Cassandra through my curls. Her mouth is still hanging open.

"Be quiet, Timmy." Summer throws a crumpled up napkin at him.

Connor mumbles something to him that I can't hear, and I only catch Timmy's response. Probably the entire cafeteria can hear Timmy's response.

"What, dude? I'm just messing around."

"Did you guys finish the social studies homework?" I know Summer's trying to change the subject, and I'm grateful.

"Omigod, I totally forgot about it." Katie jumps up so hard that her chair wobbles. "Cassandra, you didn't do it either, did you?"

"Not yet," Cassandra answers. She's still staring at Connor and me.

"We'd better get to the library. It's due tomorrow." Katie puts her hands on her hips.

Cassandra tilts her head and stares right at me. "Okay. We'll talk to you later." She stands up in a huff, and struts out of the cafeteria.

I sigh in an attempt to lighten the load that's building inside me. How many secrets can one girl have?

"I should tell Cassandra about the Spring Fling," I say, as Summer and I make our way back to the dorms.

"Yeah, you probably should." Summer reaches up and pulls a pink blossom off of a tree. She puts it to her nose and inhales. "Smell this. Isn't it awesome?"

She pushes the blossom in front of my face and I sniff. It does smell good. Like perfume. All of the trees are in full bloom now. It's so much more colorful than Los Angeles.

"When?" I ask.

"When what?"

"When should I tell Cassandra?"

Summer stops walking and looks at me. "As soon as possible."

"But I feel really bad about it." I kick a rock off the sidewalk.

"Why?"

"Because I know she likes him and—"

"Connor likes you. Not Cassandra. He didn't like Cassandra before you came here, and even if you never came here, he wouldn't like Cassandra. I tried to tell her that, but you know Cassandra—she doesn't always listen."

"I don't want to hurt her feelings," I squeak.

"It will hurt her feelings more if she sees you guys at the

dance together and didn't know about it." Summer starts walking again. "As my dad always says, the truth is hard, but the consequences of lying are even harder."

My stomach clenches. All I can hear are Summer's words over and over again in my head. *The truth is hard, but the consequences of lying are even harder.*

But what about the consequences of telling the truth? Summer will hate me. There will be no fashion show. No Spring Fling. No Connor.

In the interest of honesty, I decide to tell Cassandra about Connor. At least that only makes me a partial liar instead of a total liar.

Somehow that doesn't make me feel any better.

"I guess I should go find her." I stop walking and look around campus, as if she might pop up in front of me.

"Want me to come with you?" Summer asks.

"No, but thanks." I suddenly feel a chill, so I secure my wrap-style cardigan sweater with the bright orange button at the neckline. "This is something I have to do myself."

I turn around toward the library.

"Good luck!" Summer yells.

"Thanks," I mutter. "I have a feeling I'll need it."

# Chapter
## ★ 24 ★

CASSANDRA AND KATIE ARE SITTING AT A TABLE ON the second floor of the library. Katie's typing furiously on her laptop, a pile of books in front of her. Cassandra's looking out the window, twirling her hair.

The sight of Cassandra makes my stomach drop into my socks, but I walk toward her anyway. At least I can be honest about something.

I take a deep breath as I reach their table. "Hi, guys."

"Oh, hi, Bea." Katie smiles at me over her pile of books.

"Hey, can I borrow Cassandra for a minute?" Suddenly I don't know what to do with my hands. Putting them on my hips seems too casual. Crossing my arms seems too defensive. So they just hang there at my sides, completely useless.

Cassandra purses her lips, as if she's deciding whether

or not to talk to me. Finally she pushes her chair back and stands up.

She follows me to the poetry area, which is usually pretty empty.

"What's up?" One hand is on her hip, and her other elbow leans on the shelf. Her head is cocked to one side, and she's looking at me like she doesn't quite trust me. Which she shouldn't.

"Well, I, uhhh, I have something to tell you." I shift my weight from one leg to the other. I still don't know what to do with my hands, so I shove them into the pockets of my jeans.

"I'm waiting." Cassandra raises her eyebrows.

"I just wanted you to know that Connor asked me to the Spring Fling." I can't quite look at her face, so I stare at the *Complete Poems of Emily Dickinson* just behind her head.

She squints at me. "And you said no, right?"

"Not really." I push my hands deeper into my pockets. "I said yes."

Now both hands are on her hips, and her chin juts out over her chest. "You what?"

"I'm sorry." I finally get the nerve to look her in the eyes. "But I like him. And I guess he likes me. . . ."

"It's obvious that *friendship* means nothing to you." The words shoot out of her mouth like daggers. I flinch.

"What?" I didn't even realize we were actually friends.

Cassandra turns on her heels, and her hair whips me in

the face. "You can forget about your stupid fashion show. I was willing to help you because Summer likes you. But I knew from the minute I met you that there's something off. And now I know the truth. You are a horrible friend."

She turns the corner out of my sight.

I don't even bother to hold back the tears, which stream down my face. I wipe them with the back of my hand. It's not that I care what Cassandra thinks, because I don't. It's just that she's right.

I am a horrible friend. And a liar.

I go all the way around the library so I don't have to walk past Cassandra and Katie. I put my head down so nobody can see how red my eyes are.

Summer's at her desk when I get back to our dorm room. She jumps off her chair when she hears me come in. She takes one look at me and groans.

"Oh no. I guess she didn't take it well?"

I plop into my chair. "She hates me. And she's out of the fashion show."

Summer stands next to me and puts her hand on my shoulder. "She's angry now, but she'll get over it. I'll talk to her."

I shake my head. "She told me I'm a horrible friend."

"Don't listen to her. She's just mad because she didn't get her way for once."

I want to tell her that Cassandra's not wrong. If she knew the truth she'd totally agree.

"Don't worry," Summer says. "We'll get someone else to do the fashion show. There's going to be a line of volunteers when everyone sees how awesome your dresses are."

I smile. For the next three weeks I'll focus on the fashion show. That will take my mind off the fact that, sooner or later, the dream life I found here will come to an end, and I'll be back to being the lonely daughter of celebrities. Oh sure, I'll have people to hang out with once everyone learns who my parents are. But I won't have friends—not true friends anyway. Summer will hate me. And Connor will never talk to me again.

I shake the thought away. I decide that no matter what Cassandra says, I'm going to enjoy my fantasy life while I can.

Summer hits the shower just before eight, and my parents FaceTime me a few minutes later. For once they're actually in the same room.

"We got another e-mail about Parents' Weekend," Dad says.

"I wish we could change our schedule around." Mom purses her lips.

"Really, it's not a big deal. Please don't worry about it. I don't want you guys stressing out about this." I smile my biggest smile.

"If you're sure, Bea," Dad says. "Because if you're not—"

"I am, Dad. Really."

"Are we missing anything special?" Mom cocks her head to one side.

"No, just a rubber-chicken dinner." I never told them about the fashion show. I want to keep this part of me only for myself.

"Awwww," Dad says. "Rubber chicken is my favorite!"

I roll my eyes. "You're such a goofball."

We say our good nights, and I shut down the iPad. Even though I'm thrilled my parents won't be here to ruin my new life, I still really miss them.

# Chapter
## ★ 25 ★

$C$ASSANDRA PRETTY MUCH IGNORES ME FOR THE next two weeks. She barely talks to Summer or Katie, either, which is so unfair, since they had nothing to do with Connor asking me to the dance. But since both of them still want to be friends with me, she doesn't want anything to do with either of them.

"I feel horrible that Cassandra's blowing you off," I say to Summer while we're eating lunch. Cassandra sits with a group of seventh-graders on the other side of the cafeteria.

"She'll get over it." Summer shrugs. "And if she doesn't, then she wasn't a very good friend to begin with."

"It doesn't bother you?"

"Meh." Summer shoves the last forkful of rice and beans into her mouth.

I wish I had Summer's attitude. She doesn't care what people think or what they say. She's nearly always cheerful. I wonder how she'll feel about me after she learns the truth.

"Hey, guess what?" Summer puts her fork down. "You know Antoinette from tech class? She would totally love to be in your fashion show."

"Really?"

"Yep. Think you can make one more dress in a week?"

"Sure," I say. "I've sketched out a bunch of ideas." Sketching helps me get my mind off of stressful things. I've done a *lot* of sketching lately.

To keep my mind off everything, I throw myself into the dresses for the next week. Three of Holly's friends asked last minute if they could join in, so I spend every spare minute I have stitching and sewing, with Summer oohing and aahing over my shoulder. I even manage to squeeze in some time to make my own dress for the Spring Fling. I choose a vintage design made of white linen fabric with a rose pattern, and add princess seams for a tailored fit. I even include a boned bodice to make the skirt extra poofy (I pulled the boning out of one of Mom's old dresses years ago when she was a runway model). When I close my eyes, I can see Connor spinning me around, my dress flying out around me like a scented flower garden since I plan on spraying the hem with rose perfume for the complete Spring Fling package.

We have a quick fashion show rehearsal on Wednesday after dinner, but since the dresses aren't completely finished it's not a dress rehearsal. Summer organizes the whole thing, and everybody does a great job. They're ready for Saturday night.

I finally finish the dresses on Friday afternoon. Summer runs around campus giving them to the girls who'll be modeling them, while I put the finishing touches on my own dress for tonight's Spring Fling. I haven't even shown Summer my dress yet. It's so frilly and flowery and floofy. I'm afraid she'll laugh, and then I won't have the guts to wear it. And I really want to wear it.

Our dorm room door shoots open, and Summer flies in. "Omigod, Bea. The girls flipped out over your dresses. They're so excited to wear them."

"Really?" I'm so happy to hear this that I don't even think to hide my own dress, which is laid out on my bed. Summer looks at it and gasps.

"Is this what you're wearing tonight?"

I stare at her face for a few seconds but can't tell if she's happy or horrified. "Well, yeah, I think so. Maybe. I don't know. . . ."

Summer leaps over to my bed and touches the fabric. "It's pure awesomeness."

All the tension flies out of my shoulders. "Yeah?"

"Totally." She rubs her fingers on the hem. "You are so

amazingly talented." She breaks into a huge smile and runs over to hug me. Something inside me breaks, and I start crying like an idiot.

"Bea?" Summer takes a step back. "What's the matter?"

"Oh, Summer, I'm a horrible person." The words spill out along with my tears.

"What are you talking about?"

I can't believe I'm doing this. Two hours before the Spring Fling and I've turned into a babbling mess. Something about her hug and the way she looks at me. Summer's the best friend I've ever had. I can't lose her. I have to tell her the truth, and I have to tell her now.

"Summer, I haven't been completely honest with you." I take a deep breath and hang my head. "My parents aren't really dead." I'm surprised at how small my voice is.

Summer just stares at me for what feels like days. The words that finally come out of her mouth almost knock me over.

"I know."

# Chapter
## ✦ 26 ✦

I JERK MY HEAD UP AND LOOK AT HER. "WHAT?"

"I know."

"You know?"

"Yes. I know your parents aren't really dead." She rolls her eyes, and her head bobs up and down as she talks.

I stare at her, my mouth hanging open. I finally find the word I'm looking for. "How?"

Summer scoots back on my bed so her back is against the wall. "I've known since the weekend you stayed at my house."

I nod for her to go on.

"Remember when I went to the dentist?"

I nod again.

"They had one of those celebrity magazines in the waiting

room, so I was flipping through it. There was a picture of Zack Miller and Celestine Cruz. It looked like they were running from photographers. The caption said their daughter was with them. Her face was covered by Zack Miller's jacket, but her dress wasn't. It was a beautiful silver dress. It was your dress. I recognized it immediately."

Sarriette's. The night of my birthday.

Tears roll down my face. "You've known for all this time?"

"Yep."

"Why didn't you say anything? Yell and scream? Ban me as your friend forever?"

Summer shrugs. "I was pretty upset at first, but then I talked to my parents—"

"Your parents know?" I swallow the lump in my throat.

"Yeah. We talked about it, and they told me you'd tell me when you were ready. They figured you had your reasons."

"I did have my reasons. I was afraid if you—or anyone—knew, you'd only want to be friends with me because of who my parents are."

Summer scrunches up her nose. "Why would you think that?"

"Because that's what happened at my old school. My best friend Sophie—my *former* best friend Sophie—was only friends with me because she wanted to meet my parents. I overheard her saying it, and it was terrible."

"That's awful," Summer gasps. "Who cares that much about celebrities anyway? Aren't they just people with public jobs? That's what my dad says."

"Yes, they are, but people still freak out about them. I know now you're not like that," I blurt out. "But I didn't know when I first met you."

"Well, I'm glad you're sure now."

"You're nothing like Sophie." I pause. "So you're—you're not mad?"

"I'm not mad, really," Summer says. "But I am hurt. I understand why you didn't tell me right away, but I thought after a few weeks you knew you could trust me."

I hang my head. "I know. I'm sorry. I know you're a true friend."

"I hope you can be honest with me from now on. No more lies?"

"Never." I hold my hand up in a solemn vow, relief washing over me.

"Good," Summer says. "So what about Connor?"

"You didn't say anything to him? When you saw the picture of the dress?"

"I didn't say anything to anyone. I wanted to wait until you told me yourself. Anyway, it's not like everything about you was fake. It was just this one little part of your life, right?"

"Yes!" I jump off the bed. "Yes, that's so true, Summer. Everything else about me is totally real. Except for the fact that my parents are alive—and famous. But the rest of me is truly me."

I suddenly feel hopeful. The weight of dread has left me, and I feel like maybe I'll be able to keep my new life after all.

"Oh, Summer." I lean over and hug her. "Thank you for being such a good friend."

"You're a good friend too, Bea."

I let go of Summer and slump back on the bed. "I guess I have to tell Connor."

"Yeah, you should. The sooner the better." Summer nods.

"I know." I lie down, hands over my face. "I just don't know when to do it."

Summer looks at me sideways, eyebrows raised.

"I know I should tell him tonight, but I don't want to ruin the Spring Fling."

Summer bites her lip. "I'm not sure, Bea. . . ."

"I will tell him. Just not tonight."

"Okaaaaay." Summer drags the word out, and I can tell it's peppered with doubt. "I say the sooner the better, but it's your call."

I sit up and squeeze my eyes shut for what feels like hours while Summer gets ready for the dance. When I open my eyes, the first thing I see is my dress. I can't imagine telling Connor tonight, at the Spring Fling, while wearing that dress. I worked so hard to make it. I can't have my dream dress filled with unhappy memories. And anyway, Connor wouldn't want me to ruin the Spring Fling for him, either. We can have a great time at the dance, and then I'll tell him first thing in the morning. What's one more day?

That's it. It's decided. I'll tell him first thing tomorrow. I should feel better now that I've made a decision, but I don't. Something doesn't feel right. The pit in my stomach is getting bigger, and I swallow the lump in my throat, hoping that will fill it up—at least for the next twelve hours.

# Chapter
## ⋆ 27 ⋆

SUMMER'S WEARING MY SILVER DRESS. I SEWED ON a hot pink sash to add a splash of summer. She's spinning around in front of the full-length mirror behind our door.

"This dress is awesomesauce." She turns to the side and admires another angle.

"It really fits you." And it does. It's sparkly and sassy, just like Summer. "You should keep it."

Summer turns to look at me. "Keep it?"

"Yeah."

"Like forever?"

"Sure."

"Oh, Bea, I couldn't." She shakes her head.

"You should." I nod. "It looks way better on you than it does on me."

"You mean it?"

"Definitely."

Summer wraps her arms around me and squeezes. "Thank you."

"You're welcome." I'm happy that I could do something to make Summer happy, especially because she's been such a good friend to me.

"Now." Summer steps back. "You'd better get dressed!"

While Summer continues to admire her dress in the mirror, I step into my own dress, careful not to rip the linen. I French-braid my hair and tie it with a ribbon made from the same fabric as my dress. I'm about to put on some of Sophie's lip gloss when I stop and chuck the tube into my drawer. I don't want any reminders of my old life as Ruby, daughter of the amazing and talented Celestine Cruz and Zack Miller. Tonight, I am just Bea.

There's a knock on the door, and I almost jump out of my shoes. Summer opens it, but it's just Katie and Antoinette. Katie's flipping out over our dresses, but I don't hear much of what they're saying over the butterflies flapping around in my stomach.

Connor should be here any second.

Another knock. Summer opens the door, and there's Connor, dressed in a dark blue suit with a red tie. He's whispering something to Summer, who nods and pulls something out of a box behind the door. I can't even pretend to talk to Katie and Antoinette because they're staring at Connor, squealing and giggling and elbowing me in the side.

"Bea." Summer steps back from the door. "Connor's here for you."

I take a deep breath and walk toward him. I glance back to look at Katie and Antoinette and immediately wish I hadn't. They're not even pretending to look away. They're staring right at us.

I'm pretty sure my face is as red as Connor's tie in the three seconds it takes me to reach the door.

"Hi." I give a little wave.

"Hi." He waves back. "That's a really pretty dress. Did you make it?"

"Oh, yeah." I'm happy for the excuse to look down at my dress because at least I don't have to look at him. "Thanks."

"Here." Connor shoots out his arm and shoves a rose in my face. "This is for you."

"For me?"

"Yeah, you had mentioned that your dress had roses, so I thought it would—you know—match."

"Wow." I take the rose from him. The stem is covered in a thin plastic tube filled with water. "Thanks. It's really pretty."

Connor nods.

"I should put it down somewhere so it doesn't get ruined."

Connor nods again, and I walk to my desk as gracefully as I possibly can. I find an empty water bottle to put the flower in. Antoinette and Katie are sitting on Summer's bed staring at me with saucer-shaped eyes while Summer tries to find her shoes in her closet. It looks like she's pulling everything else out of there *except* for shoes.

"Here they are!" Summer emerges from the depths of her closet, hot pink shoes in hand.

"So, you wanna go?" Connor asks.

I glance over at Summer.

"Oh yeah, you guys go." Summer shoves a foot into her shoe. "I think I have to fix my hair again from crawling around in the closet. We'll meet you there."

"Are you sure?" I raise an eyebrow in her direction.

"Totally." She nods. "We'll see you there in a few."

"Okay," I say, and follow Connor down the hall and out of the dorm.

A group of ninth graders run past us, and then, straggling behind them, are a boy and a girl I recognize as two of Holly's friends. They're holding hands, and as much as I want to hold hands with Connor, my hand is so sweaty that his hand would probably slide right off. I never in a million years thought I'd do this, but I say a silent prayer for Connor *not* to hold my hand right now. It must work because he shoves his hands into the pocket of his suit jacket.

"So, is this your first dance?" Connor says.

"Yeah, I only went to my old school for a few months, and before that—" I stop myself before I continue my sentence.

*Before that I was tutored because I spent a lot of time on the road with my parents.*

"Before that?" Even though it's nighttime, the lampposts light up the pathway through the campus, and I can see that he's looking right at me.

"Before that I didn't go to a school that had dances."

"This is my first dance too." Connor looks down at his shoes.

We stand behind a bunch of other kids shuffling through the gym doors. When we finally get inside, I gasp.

Midcoast's gym has been transformed into a blossoming meadow. Flowers and plants line the walls, and paper vines hang from the ceiling. A silver disco ball also hangs from the ceiling, turning the air in the gym into beams of sparkles. It looks like the set of a movie, only it's real life.

"So, you want some punch or something?" Connor shoves his hands into his pockets again.

"Sure."

I scan the gym for Summer or Katie, just in case they snuck in behind us, but I don't see them. I also don't see Holly, so I jump when she calls my name from behind me.

"Whoa, Bea." Holly spins me around to face her. "That dress is so amazing."

"You really think so?" It's so important to get a real teenager's opinion of my designs.

"Totally." Holly turns to a group of girls talking behind her. "You guys, come check out Bea's dress."

I try to stand completely still as the five older girls stare at my dress. I bring my shoulder blades as far back as possible so the dress hangs nicely.

"You *made* this?" I recognize the girl from campus. Her name is Tess, I think. She's wearing a pretty silk dress, but it would be way cuter with a V-neck and a fishtail skirt.

"Yeah," I say, but it sounds more like a question since I'm not sure if she loves it or hates it.

"Spectacular." Her voice is practically a whisper, but I hear it loud and clear in my head. "I would kill to wear something like this for my cousin's wedding next month."

"I'd lend it to you, but it may not fit right." She is a good four or five inches taller than me.

"Hey." Holly bounces on the balls of her feet. "Why don't you make her one, Bea? You can have your own little side business."

"Omigod, would you?" Tess puts her hands on my shoulders. "I'll totally pay you to do that."

"Sure!" My heart is beating a trillion miles a minute. I can't believe someone, especially a high schooler, wants to pay me to design a dress for her.

"Make sure you go to Bea's fashion show this weekend. It's this year's Spotlight Project," Holly says.

The older girls are still huddled around when Connor comes back, holding a cup of punch for me. Holly gives him a huge hug, and a little bit of punch splashes in her hair.

"Look at you, handsome," Holly says. Connor's cheeks turn the color of the punch. "Did you hear that Bea's going to open up a dress shop?"

"That's awesome," Connor says. He looks at me and smiles, and now my face is the color of the punch.

Thankfully, Summer, Katie, and Antoinette run up to us at that very moment, giving my face the chance to get back to its normal color. Shane and Timmy arrive just as the band starts playing Katie's favorite song. She screams and drags us all out on the dance floor with her. We dance like crazy—until the slower music comes on—and then we go sit down. Some of the older kids stay on the dance floor for the slow songs.

The next song the band plays is a cover of the number one hit song, "Hear It from You." Katie squeals, and we're all back on the dance floor. I never paid much attention to the lyrics before, but now they're loud and clear. *Oh baby, baby, baby, we've got some talking to do. I know you're lying to me. I need to hear it from you.*

Ugh. I never did like that song.

Summer gives me a lopsided smile, and I look back at her and wince. Now that Summer knows the truth, I feel more obligated than ever to tell Connor. And I will. I just have to find the right time.

I ignore the lyrics, which seem to be screaming at me, and focus on dancing. Maybe it's the energy from the song, or the fact that we're all whirling around the dance floor, but the pit in my stomach slowly disappears. If Summer understands, maybe my other friends will too. If Summer understands, maybe Connor will understand.

"Hear It from You" ends, and the band goes into a slow song. I'm about to follow Summer and the gang off of the dance floor when Connor taps me on the shoulder.

"You, uhhhh, you want to stay and dance?" He looks at me for a minute, then looks down at his shoes.

"Oh, yeah. Sure."

The older kids are back on the dance floor, so I look at them to see how you're supposed to dance to something this slow. They look like they're doing a combination of dancing and hugging, which looks kind of nice and kind of weird. Connor takes a step toward me and puts one hand on my waist. He takes my other hand with his other hand, and then quickly drops it. He wipes his hand on his pants and then picks my hand up again. His hand is warm and a little wet, but not icky wet—more like a warm washcloth.

We sway to the music, and my heartbeat speeds up as I realize that this is my first real dance with a boy. Unfortunately, my heart isn't the only thing that speeds up. My feet do too, and I step on his toes.

"Sorry!" I step back, which causes his arm to fall off my waist.

"That's okay," Connor says. "This isn't a great song, anyway."

I force a smile. There's a sour taste in my mouth as I realize he doesn't really want to dance to the slow song. He probably wants to hang out with Shane and Summer and everyone—

"Hey, would you like to take a walk to the tennis court?" Thankfully Connor interrupts my thought.

"The tennis court?"

"Yeah, I hear they have some cool decorations out there."

"Sure, but don't you want to get back to Summer and Shane and those guys?"

Connor's smile immediately fades. "Do you?"

"No," I say. "Not unless you want to."

"No, I don't. Not right now, anyway." Connor wipes his hands on his pants again. "If it's okay with you."

"Oh yeah, it's okay with me."

We zigzag around the other dancers to the back door of the gym, which opens up to a lighted path leading to the tennis court. A bunch of other dressed-up kids run by us. When we reach the tennis court, I blink. If it weren't for the green surface, I'd never know that it's actually a tennis court. The nets are gone, and instead the court is covered with a bunch of small, white wrought-iron tables, complete with a bright bouquet of flowers in the center of each one.

The fence surrounding the court is lit up with strings and strings of white lights.

"This is amazing," I say.

"It's really cool," Connor says. We're standing next to one of the white tables. Connor looks up and points to the sky. "See the Big Dipper?"

I squint at the sky, searching for the sideways question mark.

"Just over there." Connor points up and to the right.

"Oh yeah." I clap my hands together. "I see it."

I can't believe I've never really looked at the sky before Connor pointed it out. It's so magical it almost looks fake.

"I could show you more constellations, if you want."

"Yeah, okay."

Connor doesn't answer, and I mentally slap myself in the head. Maybe he just said that he'd show me more constellations to be nice. Maybe he doesn't really want to show me more constellations at all, but I said yes, so now he's got to. Maybe—

"Bea, I just want you to know how much I like you."

I can barely hear the music coming from the gym over the sound of my heart. I didn't even know it could beat that loud.

"I like you, too." I look down at the green surface beneath my feet. Connor's looking at me, and as he does so his face is moving closer to mine. Is he going to kiss me? I think he's going to kiss me. Of course I can't be sure, because I've never been kissed before, but his face is getting awfully close to mine. I close my eyes, because that's what people do in the movies, and because I don't know what else to do.

Just as I think Connor might kiss me, a piercing scream comes from the path between the gym and the tennis court.

A group of people are walking fast toward us. At first I can't tell who they are because it's all a big blur, but then they stop and look right at us.

That's when I see the cameras.

And the flashes.

That many cameras in one place?

That can only mean one thing.

The paparazzi found me.

# Chapter
## ★ 28 ★

I GRAB CONNOR'S HAND AND RUN TO THE BACK GATE of the courts. There's lots of yelling and Connor's asking me what's going on, but my voice is frozen and I can't answer him. How did the paparazzi find me here?

I know there are woods on the other side of the courts, just past the gate, because one time during gym class I hit my ball way over the fence and had to go get it. I'm hoping we can get in there and hide before they find us.

Thankfully, it's dark outside, and the farther into the woods and away from the tennis courts we go, the darker it gets. My dress gets caught on some thorns, but I can't worry about that now. I can still hear voices, but they don't sound as close. Just to be safe, I keep going and realize I'm still holding Connor's hand.

"Bea, where are we going? Who are those people?" Connor asks when I finally stop running. I look toward the tennis courts but can't see anything except trees. I'm pretty sure we lost them.

"There's something I have to tell you—about me." I put my hands on my knees and try to catch my breath.

"Okay . . . ," Connor starts to say. He's smiling. I wish he wouldn't do that.

"It's bad."

"You're a fugitive?"

I give him a weak smile. "No."

"A foreign spy?" Connor guesses.

I shake my head.

"I know. You're a dude!"

This time I actually laugh a little.

"So if it's not any of those things, what could be so bad?"

I take a deep breath. "My parents aren't—dead."

Even though it's dark in the woods, I can see that Connor's smile is instantly erased from his face. There are tiny lines on his cheeks where his dimples were a second ago.

"What do you mean?"

"I mean . . ." I stand up straight and start pacing. "I didn't exactly tell the truth about my parents."

"You're parents aren't dead?" Connor's whole body looks limp.

I bow my head." No. They are alive and well. I never meant to lie. It just came out that way when I first met Summer and—"

"They didn't die in a car accident?"

My throat feels like it's closing up, and I tug at my necklace. "No. I'm so sorry—"

"They didn't die at all?" Connor's eyes have gone from sparkly silver to storm gray. He slumps against a tree so that every part of his body is facing downward. Except his eyes. His eyes are staring right at me.

"Please, let me explain." I stop pacing and look at him. He doesn't say anything, so I go on. I'm blurting it all out at once, quite possibly rivaling Timmy's mile-a-minute mouth. "My parents—they're Zack Miller and Celestine Cruz—and at my old school my friends only pretended to be my friends so they could meet them and of course I was devastated when I found out and I was afraid it would happen again so I told Summer I didn't have parents and somehow I said they were dead and then she told me your parents died and I felt terrible but by then it was too late to take it back so I just went on pretending—"

Connor stood up, his body now stiff as a board. "You pretended your parents were dead so we'd like you?"

"No. No, it's not like that. I pretended my parents were dead so nobody would find out who my parents really were—"

"That is sick." Connor says. "I can't believe you'd do that."

"I didn't mean to," I squeak.

"I can't believe the things I told you." Connor runs his hands through his hair. "Thoughts about my parents that I never told anybody. I thought you understood."

"I did understand," I say. "I do."

He's looking at me with an ice-cold stare, but I stumble on. "Even though my parents aren't dead, I do understand your feelings. My parents are alive, but they're away a lot and not around much like real parents—"

"Are you comparing your parents who are away a lot to my parents who are *dead*?"

"No, I just—" My voice comes out as a whisper.

"Do I even know who you are?" Connor shakes his head slowly.

"I'm still me. Nothing changed—"

"Everything changed." Connor stares at me for a second, his jaw clenched. Then, before I can say anything else, he turns and runs back toward the tennis court.

And I'm left standing in the woods, with a two-inch rip in my dream dress, alone.

I know I can't stay here long, but I can't bear the thought of facing anyone, so I slide down a tree and sit, picking pine needles off the ground. I don't know how long I'm there for, but we have a curfew, and if I'm not back on time, the whole school will come looking for me. That is, if they aren't already.

I drag myself back toward the tennis courts, which thankfully are empty. The gym lights are still on, and I can see some kids cleaning up. Instead of taking the usual sidewalk to my dorm, I lurk behind the buildings like a criminal. A criminal in a ripped linen dress.

Summer's pacing when I open the door to our room.

"Omigod, Bea, where have you been?"

I take my beat-up shoes off and fling them in the closet. Then I slump into my desk chair, and that's when the tears come. Buckets of them.

"The paparazzi found me. Well, they almost found me anyway."

"What? How?"

"Who knows?" I throw my hands in the air. "We were on the tennis courts, and I really thought Connor was going to kiss me, and then these people were coming toward us with cameras so Connor and I ran into the woods to hide and that's when I told him the truth."

"Oh, Bea." Summer looks down at the floor.

"I know. He hates me." I tug at the rip in my dress.

"I'm so sorry." Summer bites the inside of her cheek. "But I don't think those people were paparazzi."

I jerk my head up. "What?"

Summer puts her hand on my shoulder. "The local press came to take pictures of the dance and the decorations outside. They were doing a story on Midcoast. Holly told me about it when the photographers came through the dance taking pictures."

"So they weren't there for me?" I look up at her, feeling slightly sick.

She shakes her head.

I squeeze my eyes shut. I can't believe I told Connor the truth when I didn't even have to. I'm just so used to the paparazzi coming after me. I throw my hands over my eyes. How could I be so stupid?

"Maybe Connor will change his mind. Maybe he just needs some time." Summer kneels down next to my chair so we're face-to-face.

"Maybe."

But I saw the look in his eyes when I told him the truth. And I'm pretty sure he'll never forgive me.

# Chapter
## ⋆ 29 ⋆

ℬEA." I OPEN ONE EYE. SUMMER'S STANDING OVER MY bed. "Time to get up."

"Why?" I pull the blankets over my head.

"Because we have to be in the cafeteria in less than an hour for brunch."

I groan. "My stomach hurts."

"Come on." Summer pulls the blankets down. "You only have one more day to get ready. Tomorrow's the fashion show."

"Don't remind me." I pull the blankets back up.

"Bea." Summer sits down on my bed, and I scooch over to make room. "I know this is tough for you, but your dresses are awesome. They need to be seen."

I snort. Easy for her to say. She didn't just betray the nicest boy in the world.

"You can't hide in here forever." Summer pulls the covers off me.

"Yes I can." I pull the covers back up again.

"Okay." Summer picks my phone off my desk. "This calls for drastic measures." She presses a button and throws the phone in my face.

Before I know what's happening, I see Ellie looking at me in FaceTime.

"Bea?" She's squinting into the phone. "Bea, what is the matter?"

"Nothing, Ellie." I sit up in bed. "It's just—my stomach hurts."

"Did you eat something bad?"

"No."

"Then what, Bea?"

I sigh and blurt it all out. I tell Ellie about the lie, about how Connor hates me, about the fashion show, and how I couldn't invite my parents because then nobody would care about my dresses if they were there.

"Bea, why do you care?"

I blink.

"You made a mistake, lying to that nice boy. That happens. But you fixed it."

"It was a big mistake, Ellie. A big, gigantuan mistake."

"Yes, yes. It was. But Summer is still your friend, no?"

"Yes." I smile.

"And Connor . . ." She purses her lips. "His feelings are hurt. Nobody likes to be lied to."

I pull the covers over my head again, but then realize Ellie can't see me when I do that.

"So that one, you pay for," she continues. "But tell me, Bea, why do you want to do the fashion show?"

"Because I love making dresses. And Summer and Katie think they're good–"

"Do *you* think they're good dresses, Bea?"

"I–I don't know."

"This reminds me of your old friends, the mean ones."

"How?" I don't see how the fashion show has anything to do with Sophie and Damon.

"You care too much about what everybody else thinks, instead of what you think."

"Huh?"

"Those mean kids say things about you, so you run away. Okay, fine. Now something happened here, and you hide in bed. This is your one and only life, Bea. You must live it how you want."

"But I want to have friends–"

"And you do. Your true friends will stand by you. Like Summer. Your other friends, not true friends. Better you know."

"But what if everyone hates my dresses? What if they laugh at me?"

"Do you hate your dresses?"

"Of course not."

"Then who cares who hates your dresses? You do the fashion show for you. For no one else. You understand me, Bea?"

"Sort of."

Ellie sighs. "Just be yourself, Bea. Yourself, who has famous parents. Yourself, who loves to make dresses. Yourself, whose favorite color is orange. You are my beautiful, talented, one-of-a-kind Bea."

I can't help but smile. Summer's still standing at the foot of my bed, hands on her hips. She nods at everything Ellie says.

"Thank you, Ellie." I feel tears prick my eyes, but I don't want Ellie to see.

"Now, you go eat something so you will have energy for the fashion show."

"Thanks, Ellie, I will. I'm feeling a little better now."

"I am very proud of you, bubela." Ellie smiles, and Face-Time disconnects.

Summer jumps up and down, clapping her hands. "I knew a call to your nana would be just what you needed."

"You know she's not really my nana, don't you?"

"Yeah, I figured. But I could tell that you really love her, so . . ."

I hear a loud grumbling sound, and I look around to see where it came from until I realize it came from my stomach.

"Was that you?" Summer laughs.

"I guess I am pretty hungry." I push the blankets off and drag myself out of bed.

"It's blueberry pancake day," Summer says. "And you know how much we love blueberry pancakes."

My mouth actually waters at the thought of blueberry pancakes, so I throw on a pair of leggings and a long T-shirt. I look in the mirror for the first time since I got ready for the dance, and I actually scream.

"I'm a mess," I say out loud. I throw my hair in a pony-tail and pull my lip gloss out of my makeup bag. I stare at the tube, thinking about Ellie's words, and I wonder if she's right. Do I care so much about what other people think of me that I don't even know what I want anymore? I used to love lip gloss, but maybe that was because Sophie loved it. Then, when I found out Connor didn't like lip gloss, I stopped wearing it. I'm staring at the lip gloss like it's the key to all my life's secrets. Do *I* like lip gloss—or not?

Summer taps me on the shoulder. "There won't be any pancakes left if we don't get going."

I decide the lip gloss debate can wait. Pancakes are much more important right now.

Whiffs of blueberries and maple syrup hit me as we open the door to the cafeteria. And so does Connor.

I literally walk right into him.

# Chapter
## ★30★

$\mathcal{H}$E GLARES AT ME FOR A SECOND, AND THEN STORMS right past me. And right past Summer. Summer shoots me a look and I nod. She runs after him.

My stomach gurgles, but not because I'm hungry. After seeing Connor, I'm not sure I can even eat. I find a seat at our usual table while I wait for Summer to come back. Nobody looks at me funny. In fact, nobody looks at me at all.

Katie and Antoinette sit down next to me, steam coming off their tray of pancakes.

"So." Katie's practically bouncing in her seat. "How was the dance? With Connor?"

I can't bring myself to look at her, so I stare at the water glass in her hand. "It was good. Lots of fun."

"Details?" Katie leans forward so she can hear me better.

Before I can answer, Summer appears at the table, motioning for me to walk with her to the food line. "Ready to go get some pancakes?"

"You bet!" I get up so fast that my chair almost falls over.

"Sorry I took so long," she whispers once we're out of earshot of Katie and Antoinette. "It turns out Connor's got some stuff going on. I mean, *more* stuff."

"What kind of stuff?" I stop walking.

She takes a deep breath. "Remember that money his uncle was supposed to give him for the observation-deck project?"

"Yeah." I nod.

"Well, it turns out there's not enough."

"What? Why not?"

"There was less in the account than he thought. So now he can't finish the project."

"That's awful. To promise someone a gift and then not be able to—"

"That's just it," Summer says. "It wasn't a gift. The money isn't his uncle's money."

"What do you mean?"

"That money was Connor's inheritance. His parents left it for him."

I put my hand over my mouth. "Wow."

I feel like there's a golf ball in my throat. I didn't know that he was going to pay for the observation deck with his own money. Money that his parents left him. I think back to the picture of the dedication to his parents. No wonder he wanted to make sure it was included. His parents were the ones who were going to make this happen.

Holly comes up behind us. "What's up, little kids?" She puts one arm on Summer's shoulder, and one arm on mine.

Summer squiggles away. "Have you talked to Connor today?"

When Holly says she hasn't, Summer blurts Connor's whole story to Holly, who looks horrified.

"Have you told Mom and Dad?"

"No!" Summer lifts her arms in the air, and they come crashing down to her legs. "I just found out."

Holly pulls us into a quiet corner of the cafeteria, takes a cell phone out of her pocket, and presses a button. "Mom, put Dad on speaker. You're not going to believe what happened." Holly relays the entire story to them. She's on the phone for at least fifteen minutes, and I hear a lot of uh-huhs and okays. When she finally hangs up, she shakes her head.

"They said they wish they could fund the project, but they just don't have the extra cash right now."

"I know," Summer says. "It's a *lot* of money. I don't know anyone with that much extra money just lying around."

"I do," I say.

There's a pause as she stares at me. "Oh, Bea, I don't think that's a good idea. . . ." Summer begins.

"Why not? My parents have more money than they know what to do with."

"I'm not sure Connor would take it," Summer says. "He's still pretty hurt by what happened."

"I have to talk to him." I pace back and forth. "Do you think he'll talk to me?"

"I don't know." Summer sighs. "I've never seen him like this before."

"Well, I have to try. Maybe I can make it up to him. I have to offer him the money." I give a loud sniffle and nod my head.

"Okay, if you're sure it's a good—"

"I'm going to find him now."

"Want me to come with you?"

"No, thanks though. This is something I have to do on my own."

# Chapter

## ★ 31 ★

I FIND CONNOR ON THE BASKETBALL COURT. LUCKILY, he's alone. I don't think I could deal with Shane and Timmy right now. I stand there while he dribbles and shoots. He glances my way but doesn't say a word.

"Hey." I stand on the edge of the court and kick a blob of dirt off of the asphalt.

Dribble, dribble, dribble. Shoot.

"Hey," I say, a little bit louder this time.

He takes a shot and misses. After a very loud sigh, he picks the basketball up and holds it under his arm. "What do you want?"

I put my hands in the pocket of my hoodie. "I want to talk to you."

"Why?"

"Because I—I think I can help."

"What makes you think I need help?"

"Summer told me what happened."

"Whatever," Connor mumbles.

"I want to help." I practically have to yell because he's standing about ten feet away from me.

"I don't want your help." He starts dribbling again.

"But my parents can fund your project. I'm sure that they—"

"You think I'd take help from your *parents*?" He stops dribbling and throws the basketball down.

"Why not?" I say it so softly I'm not sure if he even hears me.

"You mean your *supposedly* dead parents? The parents you've been lying to me about since we met? Those parents?"

"I'm so sorry I lied to you. I really am. But I want to make it up to you."

"You can't make it up to me. And for sure you can't make it up to me by having your *very alive* parents feel sorry for me."

"It's not like that." This time I look right at him.

"It doesn't matter. I don't want *their* help." He speaks of my parents as if they're the greatest villains of all time.

"Why not? What's the difference where you get the money from, as long as you get it?"

He laughs, but it's not a ha-ha kind of laugh. "You totally

don't get it. But of course you don't. Your parents are alive!"

"Okay, so I don't get it." Now I'm getting mad. "Why don't you explain it to me, then?"

"That's just it! I shouldn't have to explain anything to you. I never had to before when you *pretended* to understand what it's like to grow up without parents."

"I know, I know. I made a huge mistake. I tried to explain to you why I did it—"

"If you really did understand, you'd know that if I took money from your parents, I'd constantly be reminded of the fact that my project was possible because of your parents, which would remind me of the fact that I'm all alone in the world. At least before, I thought I was alone with you—" He shakes his head and walks away before I can say anything else, and I'm left standing on the basketball court by myself.

I sit down on the blacktop and hug my knees to my chest. I can't blame him for not wanting to talk to me. And I definitely can't blame him for not wanting to take money from my parents. But he is acting so immature. Shouldn't he do everything he can to get that observation deck built? Doesn't he know he doesn't have to be in this alone, even if he thinks he does?

And then it hits me.

He doesn't have to be in this alone.

I leap up and run back toward the dorm. I know exactly

how to get that observation deck built—and how to win Connor back.

I will my legs to move faster.

When I finally reach the dorms, I swing the door to my room open and find Summer eating pancakes out of a plastic container.

"Did you find him?" she asks in between bites.

"Yes." I crawl under my bed and pull out my box of fabric.

"And?"

"He won't even hear me out." I carefully lift everything out of the box until I find what I'm looking for. "Aha!"

"What? What's aha? And why do you suddenly look so happy?" Summer walks toward me.

I hold up the unfinished dress, the dress that's going to solve all my problems. Then I pull out a crinkled, rolled up paper and flatten it on my desk.

Summer stares at it over my shoulder. "Holy wow."

I turn around and see that her mouth is hanging open. I have to admit. It's the most amazing design I have.

"I designed this dress for my mom last Christmas. I rolled up the sketch and tied a big velvet ribbon around it."

"She didn't like it?" Summer asks.

"She never opened it. She got a call from her agent on Christmas morning. Some work emergency. So she left. By the time she came back, she'd forgotten all about it. It was still under the tree the next week when she left for the countrywide auditions for *America's Next Cover Model,* so I packed it up."

"But you started making it?" Summer looks at the dress in my hand.

I shrug. "I thought maybe I could give it to her next Christmas."

"It's incredible," Summer says. "But how's it going to help Connor?"

"We're going to auction it off and use the money for the observation deck."

"But it's for your mom."

"She doesn't know that." My voice shakes a little.

"You think we'll get enough for it? That observation deck's pretty expensive." Summer cocks her head to one side.

"We will if supermodel and TV star Celestine Cruz models it."

"You want your parents to come to the fashion show? To Midcoast?"

"No." I shake my head. "I don't want them to. But they have to. It's the only way to save Connor's observation deck."

"But you said he wouldn't take the money from your parents." Summer raises an eyebrow.

"The money won't be coming from my parents. It will be coming from the people who buy the dress. He can't turn all of them down."

Summer's eyes get wide. "That's brilliant!"

"I know, right?"

"A website! We'll need a website so people can bid for it online."

"Can you make a website that fast?"

"Totally. You know I always get As in tech."

I rummage through my desk and hand Summer the check that I got for winning the Spotlight Project. "Here."

"What's this for?"

"The website. I can't ask you to do all this work for nothing."

"Bea." Summer raises one eyebrow. "That's what friends do."

I'm still holding the check out to her, but she ignores it.

"But–" I start to protest.

"Put that money toward the observation deck, and let's get to work." Summer opens her laptop and begins typing away. I'm suddenly grateful that Summer pays attention in tech class.

I pull out my sewing machine. I only have one chance to save Connor's observation deck. And maybe, if I'm really lucky, my friendship with him too.

# Chapter
## ✦ 32 ✦

I CAN'T WAIT UNTIL EIGHT O'CLOCK. I TEXT MY PARENTS and ask if they can talk sooner.

While I wait to hear from them, I pull the box of fabric out of my closet. I slice and sew and stitch as fast as my fingers will let me, following the specs on the design. I silently pray that my mother's measurements haven't changed much since Christmas.

While I'm busy bringing the sketch to life, Summer's working on the website so people can bid on the dress from their phones during the fashion show. She only stops to attend the Parents' Weekend dinner with her family. I don't know how long she's gone for, but she opens the door in a huff.

"Have you talked with them?" She hands me a doggie bag.

"No." I look at the time. Ten after seven. I lay my head down on the desk, careful not to touch the dress. "I'm afraid it will be too late."

"Nah." Summer shakes her head. "The fashion show isn't till tomorrow afternoon. There's still time."

I hold up the almost-finished dress. "What do you think?"

"Wow, Bea." Summer walks over and gently touches the fabric. "It's the best one yet."

"I think so too. It's simple and elegant, just like my mom."

"She's going to love it."

"I hope so. I just wonder if—"

Just then my phone rings. It's my parents on FaceTime.

When their faces appear on screen, they look panicked.

"What's the matter, baby? Are you okay?" Mom is in full makeup. She must be getting ready to do a taping.

"Sort of," I say.

"What is it?" Dad looks tired. Or maybe that's his worried look.

I take a deep breath. "I need you to be here. Tomorrow."

"Are you sick?" Mom asks.

"No." I shake my head.

"Are you in trouble?" Mom's voice is higher than normal.

"Not exactly."

"Bea, what on earth is going on?" Dad asks.

And then I start to cry.

"What is it, hon? Why are you so upset?" Mom moves her face closer to the camera.

I take a deep breath, and I tell them.

Everything. The words spew out of my mouth, like they've been waiting at a starting line behind my tongue for months, ready to sprint.

I tell them how I told everyone that my name was Bea and that my parents were dead. I tell them about Connor and Cassandra and the photographers at the Spring Fling. I tell them about the Spotlight Project and how I won. I tell them that I didn't want them to come to Parents' Weekend so that people would come to my fashion show for me—not to see them. And then I tell them that none of that matters now because Connor needs to have his observation deck funded. And I need their help.

I squeeze my eyes shut and wait for them to answer. It's quiet for so long that I worry that they hung up. I open one eye and peer at the screen. They haven't gone anywhere. It's way worse than that.

Mom is crying.

And I start to cry. Again.

"How could I not know that you design dresses? I'm your mother. And not only that, I made a living as a fashion model!" Mom dabs the tears from the corner of her eyes with a tissue.

Dad puts his hand up to the camera. He calls this a

virtual hand hold. I put my hand up to the screen so it's touching the image of his.

"So will you come?" I wipe my eyes with the back of my other hand.

Mom and Dad are having a psychic conversation. Mom's eyebrows are furrowed and Dad's lips are pursed. Not a good sign.

"It's not that easy, Bea. I'm in San Francisco. Your mother has a live taping tomorrow. Even if I didn't play tonight, I'm not sure I'd get there in time—"

The tears bubble up in my eyes again. I try to swallow them back. I don't want to upset my parents even more. This is my fault.

"I don't see how I can get out of the taping tomorrow," Mom says. "A lot of people are counting on me here. I just wish we had known sooner."

"I'm sorry," I say in a small voice. I can't even look at the camera, so I look down at my desk. A giant knot forms in my stomach.

"We're sorry, hon," Mom says. "Are you going to be okay?"

I force my head to nod. "Yeah, I'll think of something."

"Good luck, Bea." Dad smiles. "We're so proud of you."

"We really wish we could be there," Mom says.

"I know," I say.

I get off of FaceTime and look at Summer.

"What now?"

"We can still auction off the other dresses," Summer says.

"Yeah, but we'll never make enough." The knot in my stomach tightens.

"It will be a start," Summer replies.

I stare at the dress I made for Mom. For a second I think maybe one of the other models could wear it, but it wouldn't feel right.

It was made for her.

# Chapter

## ★ 33 ★

ONE HOUR TILL FASHION SHOW TIME.

Summer and I are in the auditorium setting up. We roll a red felt runner down the stage and put up signs printed with DESIGNSBYBEA.COM on them. Mrs. Kearney lets us borrow the plants from the lobby, so we line the stage with pots of flowers and greenery.

Once the stage is done, we place a program on each chair. Summer designed and typed the entire thing, and even included pictures of the models wearing my designs. The cover of the program is bright orange.

We're on the last row of seats when Holly comes in with a few of her friends.

"The decorations look great." She looks around approvingly. "Where do you want us?"

Summer leads the girls backstage to the dressing room, where all the dresses are neatly hung up, waiting for someone to breathe life into them. I stayed up late last night to put the finishing touches on Mom's dress, just in case I decide to have someone model it. Even though it was made for her, it really is special and could bring a lot of money for the observation deck.

After I finish placing the programs on the seats, I sprint to the dressing room. Summer, Katie, Antoinette, Holly, and six of Holly's friends are lined up at the mirrors, finishing up their hair and makeup. I gasp out loud when they all turn to look at me.

They look amazing.

"Are you ready?" Summer grabs my hands in hers and squeezes. Her hair is highlighted with hot pink spray, which matches the sash on her silver dress perfectly.

"You're wearing eye shadow?" I'm staring at the silver sparkles above her eyes.

"Only for you." She blinks her eyes several times. "This stuff itches like crazy."

There's a knock on the door. "Two minutes," says the voice from the other side.

Katie squeals. And then runs to the garbage can to throw up.

"Are you okay?" I sprint over to her while Summer grabs a handful of towels off the shelf.

"I think I'm nervous." Katie takes one of the towels from Summer and wipes her face. Holly drags a stool to where Katie is standing and leans her into it. "I don't feel so good."

"It's okay, Katie. Just sit here for a while." I put my hand on her shoulder. "Can I get you a glass of water?" She nods, and I grab a glass next to the sink and fill it up.

"Thank you." She takes a sip.

"One minute," the voice on the other side of the door booms.

"Are you going to be okay?" Summer asks Katie.

"I don't know." Katie's voice cracks. "Sometimes I get stage fright."

A part of me feels terrible for Katie, but another part of me wishes she had told me that before. "Don't worry, Katie. Just stay here until you feel better."

"But your dress. It's so beautiful."

"It's more important that you feel better." She gives me a lopsided smile. I can't worry about this now. We have less than a minute to get out there.

"Okay, girls." Summer claps her hands. "Let's line up, just like we practiced."

The girls are lined up within seconds, and Summer leads them down the hall to the stage entrance.

"I'll be there in a sec." I feel bad leaving Katie in here alone.

"I think I'm okay," Katie says, and takes another sip of water.

"Are you sure?" I ask.

"Yes." Katie stands up and smiles. "Let's go break a leg."

Katie runs to catch up with the other girls. Before darting backstage, I scan the audience. The auditorium is packed, but there's no sign of Connor. My heart feels heavy, until I remind myself that it's hard to recognize faces in just the light from the lobby. He might be there—maybe I just can't see him.

I line up behind the models, who are squealing and holding each other's hands. Since I'm last in line, I can't see what's happening on the stage, but I can certainly hear it. The music blares for about five seconds, and then it is lowered. A voice booms from the speakers. It's Mr. Zabar, our drama teacher–turned-emcee.

"Ladies and gentlemen, welcome to Midcoast Academy's Special Project, Designs by Bea Miller!"

Claps and cheers fill my ears. Summer peers out from the front of the line and gives me a thumbs-up. The music changes, and Summer struts onstage. The crowd goes wild, and I have to throw my hands up to my ears to dull the noise.

As the models take the stage, Mr. Zabar describes each dress in detail. I know he's reading from the cards we gave him, but if I hadn't written the words myself I never would have known. He sounds like a fashion maven.

"Summer is wearing a silver silk chiffon dress with a layer of shiny sequins lining the spaghetti straps. The hot pink sash adds a splash of color, and the hem is designed to float through the air like a silver cloud."

Summer skips across the stage so the audience can see the bottom of the dress hovering just above the runway. Even though I wore that dress before I ever came to Midcoast, it's completely obvious that it was made for Summer. Summer takes her spot on stage left, and Mr. Zabar continues in his announcer voice.

"Antoinette is wearing a knee-length royal blue strapless taffeta dress with a ruffled skirt. Silk ribbon trims the ruffles for added depth and sparkle."

Antoinette giggles as she struts up and down the runway, spinning at either end. Her skirt poofs out as she does, and the ruffles shimmer under the spotlights.

Mr. Zabar goes on to describe Holly's "metallic retro design with an asymmetrical neckline for a funky look your friends will never forget." Holly waves when she gets to the end of the runway, and the slit dolman sleeves gleam like liquid aluminum foil. I give myself a mental fist bump because that's exactly the look I was going for.

The rest of the girls take their turn on the runway, and I'm the only one left behind the curtain. I can hear my own heartbeat over the music. Any minute now Mr. Zabar is going to—

"And now, meet the designer herself, Bea Miller!"

I close my eyes and take the deepest breath ever. I

imagine myself like my mother, gliding instead of walking. Back straight. Shoulders back. Big smile. Once the image is implanted in my brain, I open my eyes and head for the stage.

As soon as I walk through the curtain, the sound hits me like a wall of bricks. People are cheering. Clapping. Yelling. I can't see anything except the lights pointed right at me. They're almost as bright as the stars outside. An image of Connor showing me the Big Dipper flashes through my mind, and I wonder if he's here. I wonder if he knows what we're about to do.

When I get closer to the edge of the stage, I can see the audience. And they're standing up! They're standing up and clapping. I look down to be sure my feet are on the ground, because I could swear I'm floating.

"Designer Bea Miller is wearing an orange cotton poplin dress with a sweetheart neckline. The sporty white buttons run down the bodice, leading into a belted, pleated skirt that's part frilly, part flirty. This design is perfect for a spring stroll, or a picnic in the park. Pair this dress with a strappy sandal for fancier occasions or with a pair of Keds for a more casual look."

The audience is still standing and clapping when Mr. Zabar hands the microphone to me. The lights dim a little bit, and the crowd gets quiet.

I squeeze the microphone tightly, leaving sweaty handprints all over it. I take a deep breath, and when I blow it out, I realize I've blown right into the microphone. I hear some giggles from the audience and come *this close* to throwing the mic back to Mr. Zabar and bolting off this stage.

But then I remember why I'm here. "Thank you so much. I, uhhh, I hope you like the dresses."

Thunderous applause.

I loosen my grip on the microphone a little bit. "All of these original designs are on sale tonight. We're having an auction to raise money for a very special project, the Jack and Diane Sullivan Memorial Observation Deck. The observation deck will be designed by Connor Sullivan, and it's going to be built off of the science room, right here on Midcoast's campus. All proceeds from tonight will go directly to this special project."

More applause.

"It's super easy to bid on the dresses. Just go to Designs by Bea dot com on your phones, and follow the instructions. The bidding will go on for the next twenty minutes. Thank you for your support."

I can't think of anything else to say, so I give the microphone back to Mr. Zabar. "Thank you, Bea! Beautiful designs for a beautiful cause. Let's take another look at them, shall we?" He then describes each dress as the model wearing it walks up and down the stage one more time. I glance over at Holly's friend Tess, who's monitoring the website just offstage. She gives me a thumbs-up, then waves me over.

"People are bidding." She scrolls through the designs on her laptop, seeing how much they're going for and who is bidding on what.

The music is still on, and the models are still strutting across the stage, Mr. Zabar enthusiastically highlighting the details of each dress yet again.

"Six minutes left," Tess says.

I stand behind her and look over her shoulder. "How much have we made so far?"

"A lot." She scrolls down and shows me the total amount bid so far.

"That is a lot." I feel hot tears stinging my eyes. "But it isn't enough."

I wonder if I should put Mom's dress on. It would probably give us an extra boost, but then I realize that I'm way too small to fit into it. As I scan the models to see who might be the same size as Mom, there's a tap on my shoulder.

"Bea, there's someone here to see you," Mrs. Kearney says.

Maybe it's Connor. Maybe he's forgiven me and he wants to support the fashion show and he's come to thank me for raising money for the observation deck. My stomach does a little jump as I picture him standing backstage.

I run one hand over my hair to smooth out the flyaways and smile at Mrs. Kearney. She steps aside and motions for me to follow her to the dressing room.

It's not Connor.

It's Ellie.

And next to Ellie are my parents.

# Chapter
## ⋆ 34 ⋆

"WE GOT HERE AS FAST AS WE COULD," MOM SAYS.

I open my mouth to speak, but no words come out.

Dad wraps me in a hug, and I breathe in his leather jacket. Every muscle in my body instantly relaxes. I feel like I'm five years old again, crawling into bed with my parents when I had a bad dream.

"So how can we help?" Mom asks.

As much as I'd like to, I can't stay in this moment forever. I pull myself away from Dad and grab Mom's dress off the hanger.

"Would you wear this?"

I gently hand her the dress. Mom holds it out in front of her and tears pour out of her eyes.

Dad's holding her hand, not saying a word, and

when I look closer, I see that he's tearing up too.

"Why are you guys crying?" Now I'm crying again. Crying is like yawning. Once someone else does it, I have to also.

Mom's shaking her head, dabbing a tissue to her eyes.

"Are you upset with me?" I ask.

"No, of course not." Mom's laughing and crying at the same time. "Why would you think that?"

"Uhhhh, because I told everyone you were dead?"

Now Dad's half laughing, half crying.

"Bea." Dad kneels down next to me. "You're such a great kid, and you're turning into a wonderful young woman. Despite us, I think."

"What do you mean?"

Mom's back on the stool next to me. "What Dad's trying to say . . ." Mom swallows. "We haven't been the best parents, hon. And we're really sorry."

Oh boy. Now she's sobbing. And it's all my fault.

"No! Mom, Dad, that's not what I think—"

"We know you don't, Bea." Dad takes my hand. "And that's what makes you so special. You never once thought that maybe we were the problem. But we were. We are."

"No, you're great parents." I squeeze Dad's hand.

"We love you very much." Dad squeezes back. "But we could do better."

"We could be involved more," Mom adds. "We *will* be involved more." She and Dad are having one of their psychic conversations, and he's nodding as she talks.

"I'm really sorry. About the dresses. I just never knew—" Mom stifles a sob. "I just never knew that you had this amazing talent. I guess I was too wrapped up in my own stuff."

"We both were," Dad says.

"Well, you guys have important jobs."

"Listen to me." Mom's dark eyes look directly at me. "Nothing is more important than being your parents."

There's a knock on the dressing room door, and Tess peeks her head in. She does a double take when she sees my parents, but then her eyes fall back on me.

"Three minutes thirty-five seconds," Tess says.

"Go." Mom unzips her jacket. "We'll meet you backstage."

I throw off my shoes and hold them in my hands (only Mom can run in heels), bolt out of the dressing room, and slide down the hall in my stockings. I arrive at Tess's side just as the music's ending, then I slip back into my shoes, floof my hair, and, as gracefully as possible, walk onstage toward Mr. Zabar.

Mr. Zabar's obviously a professional, because he looks at me as if I was supposed to be there. "Ladies and gentlemen, Bea Miller!"

The crowd cheers again, and if I wasn't so distracted, I probably would have turned as red as the runway.

I take the microphone from Mr. Zabar, and the crowd quiets down.

"Thank you." I'm holding the microphone too close to my mouth, and the feedback makes my ears vibrate. I bring the microphone down to chest level and try again. "Thank you. It's so nice of you all to come and bid on these dresses. As you know, we're raising money for an amazing observation deck to be built right here on campus. This is an important project to me, and to my friends." I motion to the models who are lined up next to me.

"Another thing that's important to me is my family. Sometimes I forget that because—well—because my family isn't like most families. And that's why it's not always easy to talk about it. . . ." I stop and look at the audience. Now that the house lights are on, I can see the entire auditorium. Summer's parents are seated a few rows back, and I almost drop the microphone when I see Connor sitting next to them.

"I know now that families aren't all the same. Some families aren't even families at all. They're really good friends who become your family, who take care of you like family. And that counts too." I stare right at Connor, but he doesn't look at me at all. His program is open in his lap, and he's leafing through it.

"On this special day, I'd like to introduce you to my family." Whispering fills the auditorium, and almost everyone starts looking around. "Ladies and gentlemen, please welcome my dad—Zack Miller."

Dad enters from stage left, at which point the entire room bursts out in applause and whoops and cheers. I can barely hear what he says when he comes up and hugs me.

I peek around him to where Mom is waiting backstage. She's wearing her dress, and my jaw becomes unhinged from the rest of my face when I see her because I've never seen her look so amazing. This is what happens when fashion wears a person, instead of a person wearing fashion.

I whisper to Dad and give him the card that I made up about the dress—just in case. Then I hand him the microphone.

"Ladies and gentlemen," he begins. "Our feature design is worn by my wife, the one and only Celestine Cruz!"

Mom struts down the runway, smiling and waving to the crowd. The audience is on its feet, stamping and clapping and screaming loud enough to drown out the music. I glance at my models, who are looking somewhat shell-shocked. I guess I'll have some explaining to do.

As soon as Dad starts talking, you could hear a pin drop. "This vintage-inspired, sleeveless, lace overlay has a gorgeous silver grosgrain ribbon at the waist. Sequins line the fitted bodice for the look that will make you shine brighter than the brightest star."

Dad continues to read from the card, and Mom walks back and forth on the runway, spinning and twirling and giving the crowd quite a show. Cell phones are out and flashing, capturing the star power of Mom and Dad. After Dad reads all the words on the card, I whisper in his ear, and he nods.

"Ladies and gentlemen, bidding on this divine creation will last for ten minutes. So get those phones ready. The highest bidder will not only receive this spectacular dress worn by Celestine Cruz, but you'll be giving the kids here at Midcoast a gift that will serve them for years to come."

The Zack Miller smile lights up the stage. "And as an extra bonus, Celestine and I would be honored to treat the winning bidder to dinner. Restaurant of your choice!"

I look at Dad and cock my head. That wasn't in the script. He winks.

Tess gives me the thumbs-up from backstage, and I nod to Dad.

"Okay, folks. Bidding is open!"

The glow from cell phones lights up the room. The music starts up again, and Mom continues with the runway walk, this time escorted by Dad. As they walk past the other models, Mom and Dad give each of them hugs.

I sneak backstage to find Tess frantically typing on the laptop.

"Good gravy," she says. "We're racking in a ton of cash here. It's gone crazy!"

I look over her shoulder. "How much time left?"

"Three minutes four seconds."

I stand there staring at the screen. It's moving so fast that I can't even see what the bids are.

"You're not going to believe this." Tess scrolls through open tabs on the laptop. "We're getting bids from outside of school."

"What?" I squint at the computer. "What does that mean?"

Tess smiles. "It means the auction's gone viral."

More numbers scroll in, and Tess never takes her eyes off the screen.

"How much time do we have?" I bite my fingernails.

"Less than one minute. The bids are still pouring in. And not just for that one dress. The bids are going higher for *all* the dresses."

I peek out of the curtain and hold both hands up. Somehow Dad knows what I mean. Maybe my parents' psychic conversations are rubbing off on me.

"Ten seconds left to bid!" Dad yells into the microphone.

"Whoa," Tess says.

"What?" I hover over her.

"That's it!" She sits back and takes a deep breath. "Here's the winning bid. And it came from someone here at Midcoast."

She shows me the number on the screen, and I stumble backward. It's a big number.

I practically skip to the stage and take the microphone from Dad.

"The winning bidder is Denise Sholl." A lady from the audience stands up and shrieks.

"Come on up here, Denise." Dad holds his arms out for a hug. I'll bet Denise never ran so fast in her life.

"Congratulations to Denise," I say into the microphone. "And thank you, all of you. Because of you, Midcoast Academy will be lucky enough to be home to the Jack and Diane Sullivan Memorial Observation Deck."

The crowd is on its feet again. I scan the heads of the audience, eager to see Connor's reaction. I find Veronica and Eric, but the chair next to them is empty.

Connor is gone.

# Chapter
## ★35★

ALL THE MODELS GATHER BACKSTAGE AFTER THE fashion show.

I introduce my parents to my friends, who are freaking out a little. I think Katie might puke again. She pulls me aside.

"Why didn't you tell us? I thought you didn't have parents!"

"I'm really sorry." I purse my lips, trying to figure out how to explain. "It's just that kids at my old school only pretended to like me because of my parents, and I was afraid it would happen again."

Katie doesn't say anything for a minute, but her eyebrows are pinched, so I can tell she's thinking.

"I guess I understand that," she finally says.

"Thanks." I smile.

"Eeek! Your dad is so cute." She's bouncing up and down, takes one look at me, and then stops, folding her hands in front of her.

"It's okay, Katie. You're allowed to be psyched to meet them."

"Oh good, because I totally am." Then she lets out a squeal and joins the other girls.

After apologizing to the other models for the big surprise and giving the same explanation I gave to Katie, I leave them to change out of their dresses. I walk Mom, Dad, and Ellie to the lobby. They've been traveling for the past twelve hours, and they're exhausted. I know they want to go to their hotel and collapse.

"Thank you for doing this," I say as I hug Mom. "I'm sorry you had to cancel your taping. I know a lot of people were counting on you."

Mom touches my nose. "*You* were counting on me."

After Dad gives me a huge bear hug, Ellie takes my hand.

"You should be proud, bubela."

"Thank you, Ellie." And I don't just mean for the nice compliment. I hug her as tight as I can, and they walk outside toward their waiting limo.

"See you tomorrow!" I yell, and I don't even care who sees me waving to a limousine.

I collect my friends back at the dressing room, and we make our way to the cafeteria to grab a snack.

Within seconds of walking through the doors, I'm being swarmed. Kids I don't know are pushing and shoving to talk to me.

"I can't believe your dad is Zack Miller," Timmy gushes.

"Yeah, I thought your parents were dead or something," Shane says.

Before I can answer, Holly and a bunch of her friends have become my Midcoast bodyguards.

"Give her some space," Holly yells. "Sheesh."

"Yeah, let the poor girl get some food," Tess chimes in.

Holly winks at me, and she and Tess shoo most of the kids away, whispering as they go.

"Thanks for that," I say.

"Of course. I don't know why people are making such a big deal."

And this is why I love Summer and her family.

"Have you seen Connor?" Summer asks Holly.

"No, but that was really nice what you guys did for him."

I hope he thinks so.

After things calm down a bit, Summer and I join the end of the food line. Kids are definitely looking at me differently. In fact, they're definitely looking at me, period. Which isn't something they did much of before today.

Just as we're close enough to place our order, I feel a tap on my shoulder.

"Hi, Bea." It's Cassandra, with a huge grin on her face.

She's got one hand on her hip and the other hand is holding a gold Coach clutch, which is a fabulous bag, but it completely clashes with what she's wearing.

"Uhhhh, hi." If she hadn't said my name and tapped me on the shoulder, I would have sworn she had me mistaken for somebody else.

"So listen." Cassandra touches me lightly on the arm. "About that whole Connor thing. I'm really sorry I made such a big deal out of it. It's so totally obvious that he likes you and not me."

She's being very nice to me. Too nice.

"So, can you forgive me? Friends again?"

Before I can think about responding, my thoughts are flooded with Sophie and what I overheard that day at my party. *How long do I have to act like Ruby's best friend?*

All of a sudden Cassandra has Sophie's face. But instead of feeling angry or upset, I feel perfectly calm looking at her. I know exactly why she's being nice to me today, when she hated me yesterday. "I'd like to be your friend, Cassandra, but only if you want to be friends with me."

Cassandra flashes a lip-gloss-coated smile. "Of course I want to be friends with you."

"Are you sure it's me you want to be friends with, and not my parents?"

"What is that supposed to mean?" Cassandra's lips get pouty.

"It means that I'd like to be friends, but you may never meet my parents. You'll be friends with me. Not them."

"But if we're friends, I'll meet your parents *eventually*."

"Maybe not. Is that okay?"

Cassandra's smile is gone, and she's back to giving me her usual glare. "Why are you making such a big deal of this?"

"I just want to make sure that you want to be my friend for the right reasons."

"And so because of that you're banning me from meeting your parents?" Her voice is higher and louder than it normally is. "What about Summer? Is she not allowed to meet your parents either?"

"Summer wanted to be my friend long before she found out who my parents are."

"Yeah, well, you didn't steal Summer's boyfriend," Cassandra says under her breath.

Summer rolls her eyes. "He was never your boyfriend, Cassandra. He—"

"It doesn't matter." The words fly out of Cassandra's mouth like daggers. "It seems Bea doesn't understand that friendship is a two-way street."

"We can start over," I say. "Friends? True friends?"

Cassandra flips her hair. "Can I meet your parents?"

This tells me all I need to know, so I shake my head. "I'm really sorry."

"You know what? Forget it." Now Cassandra has both hands on her hips. "I wouldn't want to be your friend anyway. I'm glad Connor finally knows the truth about you."

I smile. "So am I."

# Chapter
## *36*

I SPEND THE NEXT DAY SHOWING MY PARENTS AND Ellie around town. We visit the bookstore, the harbor, and the ice cream shop. Of course people whisper and point, and some even stop to chat, but mostly, everyone leaves us alone.

Summer's parents invite us over to dinner, and my parents are so fascinated with town that they decide to walk there.

"So, Bea." Dad puts his arm around me as we walk. "Your mom and I are kind of in love with this place."

"Yeah, Midcoast's pretty great."

"And so is Maine. Everybody's been exceptionally nice. We're thinking about getting a house here," Mom says.

"What?" I stop in my tracks.

"Yeah, like a vacation home." Dad takes a deep breath. "To get away from it all."

"And, of course," Mom adds. "To spend more time with you."

"Really?" I look from Mom to Dad.

"What do you think about that?" Dad asks.

A few weeks ago I would have been totally horrified at the thought. But now I feel all warm and gooey inside. Like I just had a cup of hot chocolate—with marshmallows.

I can't wait to tell Summer.

Which I do as soon as she opens the door. I don't even make it past the entryway of their house when I start blabbing. She listens politely, but her eyes keep darting around the room. I'm not sure she's hearing a word I'm saying.

"Didn't you hear me? My parents want to get a house here."

"I know, Bea, and that's awesome. It's just that I have to tell you—"

"Dinner's ready," Veronica calls from the kitchen.

"Just a minute," Summer calls back.

Eric comes in and ushers us forward. "Come on, girls. This is a very important night."

I raise an eyebrow at Summer. I didn't think her family would make such a big deal about having my parents over for dinner. I thought they were too cool for that.

It's obvious that we're not eating on the couch tonight.

Tonight we're in the dining room. The table is set for nine. I wonder if Holly has a friend over.

Summer and I sit at one end of the table, and Mom, Dad, and Ellie are at the other end. Eric and Veronica are loading the table with plates of food. My mouth waters at the smells wafting from the dishes.

The front door opens, and Holly's voice echoes through the house. "Sorry we're late."

"You're just in time," Veronica says. "Wash your hands and take a seat."

A minute later Holly bounces into the dining room.

Followed by Connor.

Veronica introduces my parents and Ellie to Holly and Connor. Connor smiles politely at them but never looks at me.

"I'm so glad you could all join us here tonight," Veronica says once she sits down.

"Thanks for having us," Mom says. "Everything smells delicious."

"I hope it is." Veronica picks up her glass. "But first, a toast. And an announcement. Or, an announcement, and then a toast." She lets out a nervous giggle.

I look at Summer, but she doesn't meet my eyes. She's got a big goofy smile on her face, though. We all pick up our glasses and stare at Veronica, whose hand is shaking so much that her wine is sloshing around in her glass, threatening to spill over the top.

"This is a pretty big day for us." She smiles at Eric, but her voice is as shaky as her hand. I can't believe she's making such a big deal of meeting my parents.

Eric waits for her to go on, but she can't seem to get the words out. "We wanted you all here to be a part of this."

I glance over at Holly, who's positively beaming. Then I sneak a peek at Connor, who looks as confused as I do.

"Connor." Eric turns to face him. "There's something we'd like to talk with you about."

"Okay." Connor's eyes dart from Eric to Veronica.

"We would like it very much if you would become an official member of our family."

Connor's chin practically touches the table.

"We spoke with your uncle," Eric continues. "We know you haven't had the best relationship with him, and he agreed that we're better equipped to raise kids than he is. So—"

Eric looks at Veronica and nods.

"So we'd like to adopt you." Veronica's eyes are teary. "If that's okay with you."

Connor's still holding his glass in the air. He doesn't move or say anything for what feels like hours. Finally, he puts his glass on the table and looks at Eric.

"Are you serious?"

"Yes, Connor. We are very serious."

"I'd live here?"

"You'd live here."

"For real?"

"If that's what you want."

I think everyone at the table is holding their breath. I know I must be turning blue by now.

Connor breaks out into a big smile, dimple and all. "I'd really like that."

Veronica puts her glass down, scoots out of her chair and over to his, and wraps her arms around his shoulders.

"Welcome to the family."

Eric gets up next, and Holly and Summer follow. They pull him into a group hug, while Mom and Dad sit across from them, clapping.

More than anything, I want to give Connor a hug too. But he hasn't spoken to me in days.

"Let's eat," Eric says when everyone's back in their seats.

The food is incredible, and Mom and Dad talk with Veronica and Eric like they've known each other for years. They don't talk about Hollywood. They don't talk about major league baseball. They just talk. Holly, Summer, and I talk, and Holly, Summer, and Connor talk, but Connor and I don't say one word to each other.

After dinner Veronica calls us into the family room. "There's one more thing we'd like to do."

Eric pulls a wrapped box out of the closet.

"This is for you." He puts the box in front of Connor.

Connor stares at it, until Summer jumps in. "I'm going to open it if you don't."

Connor tears open the wrapping paper to reveal a box with a picture of a telescope on it.

His eyes are almost as big as the box. "Is this—is this the Celestron NexStar Eight SE?"

"It is." Eric smiles.

Connor picks the box up. "But it's empty."

"That's because the telescope is already set up outside." Eric points to the backyard. "We thought you could use it here until the observation deck's ready."

"I can't accept it." Connor shakes his head and pushes the box away from him. "It's too much."

"Nonsense," Veronica says. "Just think of it as a gift for all of the birthdays we missed before we knew you."

I'm holding my breath, waiting for Connor to say something. He goes from staring at the telescope box to staring at Eric and Veronica.

"Thank you." He says it so quietly I have to strain to hear him.

"There's something else." Veronica hands Connor a large envelope.

"I can't accept—" Connor begins to protest.

"Please," Veronica says. "It's important to us that you do."

Connor nods and carefully tears open the top of the

envelope. He pulls out a parchment certificate with a gold seal at the bottom. I can't read what it says, but Connor's silver eyes get all watery.

"You named a star after my parents." His voice is soft.

"We thought you needed something to look at through your telescope," Eric says.

"We know how important they are to you." Veronica dabs her eyes with a tissue. "And even though you're part of our family, you're also part of theirs. We never want you to forget that."

Connor's staring at the certificate, his eyes filling up. He wipes them with the back of his hand.

I swallow the star-size lump in my own throat and glance over at Mom. She's welling up too.

"How about we check it out?" Eric stands, breaking the silence in the room.

Eric puts his hand on Connor's shoulder and leads him out to the deck. The telescope is set up next to the grill. The sky is clear and dark, and the stars are amazing enough without the telescope. I spot the Big Dipper immediately and want to tell Connor that I found it all by myself, but the words get stuck in my throat. He won't want to hear it anyway.

Everyone takes turns looking through the eyepiece—except for me. Connor's standing next to the telescope, and I don't want to ruin this for him. But when it's Mom's turn,

Connor is eager to help. He tells her where to look and even where to stand. I giggle. It's funny watching my mother be so clueless. It's something I haven't seen very often.

"Is it cool enough for some hot chocolate?" Veronica pulls her sweater tight.

"It's always cool enough for hot chocolate," Summer says.

"I'll get some started," Veronica says.

"Let me help," Mom chimes in. I giggle again, wondering if my mom even knows how to make hot chocolate.

Holly, Eric, and Dad are still huddled around the telescope. Summer and I take a seat on the lounge chairs. We just stare at the stars for a little while. The sky is mesmerizing.

"Pretty cool, huh?" Summer smiles. "Connor's going to be my brother."

"That's awesome," I say. "Your parents are the best."

She nods, and then looks at me, all serious. "Your parents are pretty great too, you know."

I purse my lips. "They really are."

"So." Summer motions to Connor. "Are you guys ever gonna talk again?"

I shrug. "That's not really my decision."

"Yeah, well, if your parents do get a house here, we'll be spending a lot of time together. And it wouldn't be good if my BFF and my brother didn't get along." Summer wiggles her eyebrows, and her lips curl into a smile.

"Who's ready for hot chocolate?" Veronica asks, and Summer jumps out of her chair.

"That sounds pretty good right now." Dad rubs his arms. "I guess I'm not used to this brisk weather yet."

Eric slaps him on the back. "Come on in. Let's get you thawed out."

They laugh all the way to the door, Summer on their heels. Before she closes the door behind her, she gives me a wink and then motions to Connor.

Connor and I are the only ones left outside.

We are alone.

# Chapter
## ⋆ 37 ⋆

CONNOR'S FIDDLING WITH THE TELESCOPE, AND I'M sitting on the edge of the lounge chair. I have to talk to him. It's now or never.

I scoot off the chair and slowly walk over to where he's standing.

"This is pretty awesome." I point to the telescope.

"Yeah." He's looking through the eyepiece, adjusting something.

"I mean, the whole night's been pretty awesome. You know, how you're going to be part of Summer's family and all." I stick my toe in between the slats of wood on the deck.

"I know. I can't believe it." He's still messing with the telescope.

"What are you doing?" I am a little curious, but mostly I'm just trying to make conversation.

He holds up the certificate in one hand, looks through the lens, and tweaks something on the telescope with the other hand. "Looking for this star."

I don't say anything, just shove my hands in the pockets of my hoodie. I look up. There are tons and tons of stars. I don't know how he's going to find one out of the trajillion that are up there.

"There it is." He's still looking through the lens.

"You found it?" I look up at the sky.

"I think so. It gives the coordinates."

He looks for a while longer, then stands up.

"Wanna see?" He takes a step back.

"Really?" I shove my hands deeper into my pockets.

"Sure." He shrugs. "I mean, if it weren't for you, we wouldn't even have an observation deck for this telescope, so—"

"No, it wasn't me. It was everyone. Summer, Holly, and the whole school."

"Yeah, I know." Connor looks at his feet. "But it was your project, so thanks."

I take a deep breath. My heart is beating so fast. Maybe that's why my words spill out just as quickly. "I'm so sorry, for lying to you. I know I can never make it up to you, but I hope one day you'll forgive me."

Connor looks at me for a split second, then he looks at the telescope. "So are you gonna take a look?"

I swallow the lump in my throat and step up to the eyepiece.

The stars look a lot like they look without the telescope, only they're much bigger and much, much twinklier. It looks like they're dancing.

Connor steps in beside me and bends down so he's at the same level as I am. My heart speeds up, and I take a deep breath to try to slow it down. "That's it. That's the Jack and Diane Sullivan star."

"It's beautiful," I say. And it is.

"Yeah," Connor says. "It's a good one."

I stare at it for a little while longer, until I hear Connor chuckle. I jerk my head up to see what's so funny. But he's just standing there, looking at the sky, laughing.

"What?" I ask.

"It's just that—" He shakes his head, but he's still smiling. "Now both our parents are stars."

I give him a lopsided smile. I've really missed the sound of his laugh. "I'm happy for you. I mean, I know nobody can replace your parents, but now you have a whole other family."

"I'm pretty happy for me too." Connor smiles, and for the first time in a long time, I can see his dimples.

"Think we could be friends again?"

Connor shrugs. "I don't know. Maybe someday."

My stomach sinks a little and I nod.

And then I see it.

A shooting star.

I squeeze my eyes shut and make a wish. And then I know. Connor and I will be friends again someday.

I peek through the window to where Mom and Dad are laughing and sipping hot chocolate with Eric and Veronica. Summer is chatting with Holly, Topaz curled up at her feet. And even though Connor hasn't quite forgiven me yet, I'm still here, with him, looking up at the most sparkly sky I've ever seen.

No secrets. No fake friends. Just me, Connor, and the stars. And families who love each other.

Best. Night. Ever.

# ★ Acknowledgments ★

$\mathscr{F}$IRST OF ALL, I'D LIKE TO THANK YOU, AWESOME reader! I'm grateful you chose to share your time with Ruby and friends.

A huge thank-you to my wonderful editor, Alyson Heller, and the entire team at Aladdin/Simon & Schuster. Ruby and I couldn't have landed at a better home. And another giant thank-you to my magical agent, Sarah Davies. Thank you for believing in me. I'm forever grateful that you pulled me out of the slush pile, and I feel lucky to walk the publishing path with you by my side.

Thanks to cover artist Lucy Truman, who brought Ruby to life so brilliantly.

I can't give enough thanks to my critique group, the talented and insightful MGBetaReaders. This book is better than it would have been because of you. You're all spectacular. I'd especially like to thank the readers for this manuscript: Jen Malone (such a wonderful friend and mentor to all newbie writers), Brooks Benjamin, Jeff Chen, Jean Giardina, and Karen Hallam, and query/early chapter readers Ella Schwartz, Melanie Conklin, Dana Edwards, Gail Nall, Rebecca Sutton, Chris Whitaker, Becky Appleby-Sparrow, and Ki-Wing Merlin. Big thanks also to my friends who read early versions: Stephen DeBock (my middle-school language arts teacher who is still teaching me after all these years!), Jane Coloccia, Rich Hoffman, Margaret Hoffman, Krissy Huetz, Susan Ilias, Rona Cherry, Madonna Kilcollum, Sean Dowd, and Michael Barron. Thanks also to my friend and writing teacher Jenny Milchman, who assured me I would get here someday soon.

I owe a debt of gratitude to SCBWI for helping all new writers learn their craft. And to the Camden Public Library in Camden, Maine, for being the most inspiring writing place ever.

And of course, big thanks and hugs to my young readers Ethan Hoffman, Maia Hoffman, Cole Huetz, Sierra Moench, Reese Barron, and Sophie Frank. Your enthusiasm encouraged me to keep going! I write for you.

The biggest thank-you of all goes to my family. To my parents, Lew, Joy, Ron, and Bonnie, for reading every single page and enthusiastically calling me with your thoughts. Thank you for teaching me that I could do anything I put my mind to (I won the parents jackpot). And to my mother-in-law, Marianne Buehler, for sharing your thoughts on publishing and allowing me to share my pages with you (I also won the in-law jackpot). To my husband, Josh, thank you for your unwavering belief in me and my writing. I honestly never would have started if you didn't believe I could do it (see . . . I do listen to most of what you say)! And of course, thank you to my kids, Hallie and Morgan. Thank you for sharing your favorite books with me. Thank you for reading everything I write, and thank you for letting me stalk you and your friends for story ideas (you do know about that one, right?). But mostly, thank you for giving me the most important job of all . . . being your mom.

I am grateful for all of you. Your love and support wrote this book.

# Check out these great titles from Aladdin M!X:

## ALADDINMIX.COM